UNDERCOVER CRUISE

A Maggie McFarlin Mystery

Charisse Peeler

CONTENTS

For
My Husband
Michael Alan Peeler

FRIDAY

CHAPTER 1

Maggie had been on the road for almost ten hours. Her right leg had cramped because she refused to use the cruise control. She was still sixty-two miles from Salisbury, where she had already reserved a room at the Courtyard.

Only a few months had passed since she'd last seen Mike Marker, the former Palm Beach County detective. Their occasional texts and phone calls were nice, but she was looking forward to seeing him in person.

Hurricane season meant road trip for Maggie. She spent a week in Nashville for Hurricane Ivan and two weeks in Panama City for Hurricane Loren. Two weeks without electricity was not an option at her age or her level of tolerance.

This time it wasn't a hurricane pushing her to drive north but an invitation to spend some time at her friend's cabin in the Smoky Mountains. And why not? She had never been there and it was the perfect excuse to stop by and see the handsome detective.

Maggie wasn't sure what her relationship with Mike was —friends for sure, with just a bit of harmless flirting and liking each other's Facebook posts. Any real hope for anything other than a long-distance friendship had pretty much vanished when Mike retired and moved 731 miles back home to Salisbury... and the fact he was now responsible for his fourteen-year-old daughter.

The miles continued. Finally, when Maggie was less than

ten miles away, she stopped one last time to gas up and let her nerves settle. She was also hungry; her last meal was an egg muffin at five o'clock that morning, when she left Boca.

As the pump worked, she pulled out her phone and texted Mike her ten minute arrival. Mike's response was instant. He lived close by, and he would meet her at the hotel. She would have no time to freshen up.

There were plenty of open parking spots when she arrived at the hotel, so she picked one closest to the front entrance, but before she got out, she ran a brush through her tangled hair. She used the rearview mirror to look at the result, but she only saw dark circles under her eyes.

She grabbed her pocketbook from the passenger seat and got out, stretching her back as she walked through the automatic doors. She headed straight to the woman standing at the reception counter. Then she awkwardly dug in the front pocket of her bag, finally finding her Florida driver's license and credit card. She handed them to the woman.

"I think he is waiting for you," the woman said, pointing behind Maggie.

Maggie turned. "Mike," she said, smiling, "I walked right past you."

"You did," Mike said, placing his strong arms around her then bringing her in for a hug.

She closed her eyes and took a deep breath, taking in the remnants of his aftershave and feeling safe for the first time in a long time. That is what Mike did for her; he made her feel safe. She finally let go when their embrace became too awkward.

"You look great," she said, "been hitting the gym, I see." She stood back an arm's length to admire the six-foot tall former detective.

He looked right back at her with a wide smile and those amazing blue eyes that felt like they could pierce your soul. He had lost his Florida tan but a charismatic glow still surrounded him. Butterflies tickled Maggie's insides.

"Well, you are definitely a sight for sore eyes," he said,

looking her up and down, making her more aware of her own thick middle and her menopausal mustache she hadn't waxed in three weeks.

Maggie shifted her gaze. She noticed the woman behind the desk patiently waiting, holding out the small envelope with her key card and internet password. The woman was watching them with amusement.

Maggie walked over and took the small package. "Thank you," she said, noticing the woman had given her two key cards instead of just one.

"Have a nice time." The woman smiled, tilting her head toward Mike.

Maggie blushed and turned back to Mike, He was still watching her, his arms folded across his chest.

"How is the cat business?" Maggie asked, hoping to distract him.

"Funny you should ask," Mike said, smiling wide. "I found a lost dog just this morning. The reward was fifty bucks, increasing our dining options. We can even afford Applebee's for dinner if you would like."

"So there's an Applebee's nearby. Good to know I haven't totally left civilization." Maggie paused to make sure she hadn't offended Mike. "I'm starving. Is there a local favorite nearby?"

"I have the perfect spot." Mike smiled again. "Definitely local."

"Hopefully, they have more than tapas," Maggie said, feeling the rumbling in her stomach.

"'Tapas'—as in small plates of food, right?" he asked, narrowing his eyes.

"Yes, what else would I be talking about?"

"Boy, are you in for a big surprise." He motioned her to follow him.

"I love sampling local cuisine," Maggie said as Mike opened the car door to let her in. Maggie detected a bit of a southern accent in Mike's voice that she had never noticed in Florida.

After driving for not much more than a mile, Mike pulled into the dirt parking lot of a small shack-like building. The sign hanging in front of the building read *Shake Shack*. A large covered front porch area with several long picnic-style tables took up most of the space in front of the building. The screen door creaked as they walked in, slamming hard behind them. They walked directly to a rustic counter, where a middle-aged woman greeted them with a big Southern smile. Several small tables lined one of the walls, but the majority of the seating was outside.

Behind the counter, a shoulder-high pass-through separated the grill in the kitchen from the customer area. Hand-painted signs displaying the menu options hung on the wall above the pass-through.

"What are you having?" Maggie asked Mike, hoping for some insight.

"They have a great chicken sandwich."

"That sounds good," she said, looking over the short drink menu.

Mike ordered chicken sandwiches and Cheerwine for both of them. The woman behind the counter wrote the order on a small pad, tore off the page, and placed it on a clothespin. The fry cook pulled it to the other side and began grilling. Mike handed the woman a few bills.

"Keep the change," Mike said as he pulled open an old-fashioned cooler next to the register. He pulled out two bottles and motioned Maggie to the door. They sat across from each other at the end of one of the long tables. Mike handed Maggie her bottle. She looked at it, confused.

"What's the matter?" Mike asked.

"Cheerwine?" Maggie held it up. "Is there actually any wine in it?"

Mike laughed. "You never had a Cheerwine?"

"I never even heard of it," she said, shaking her head. She twisted off the top and took a drink as Mike watched her.

"What do you think?" he asked.

"Sweet...but refreshing. It tastes like a cherry cola. If it had wine in it, it would be even better. Don't you think it's false advertising?" She smiled, holding the bottle up.

"It's a Southern thing," he said, tipping back his bottle. He finished the last of his drink just as the woman who had taken their order delivered their sandwiches.

"Have you been doing any writing?" Mike asked.

"Not really. I'm still struggling with the creative side of my brain, but I did sign up for an online course to become a certified private investigator."

Mike nodded. "I'm impressed."

"The only thing is, I'll have to work two years with a licensed P-I before I can be independent...but I did get this." Maggie fumbled through her wallet then pulled out her concealed weapons permit and laid it on the table.

"Now I *am* impressed." He paused. Suddenly his face looked panicked. "You aren't carrying now, are you?"

"No, Mike, but North Carolina is a reciprocal state, so technically I could carry. But I didn't bring it, because what if I decide to drive into a state that doesn't reciprocate."

"Smart girl," Mike said, relieved. "Did you give up writing entirely?"

"No, I still do some technical writing once in a while, but I've turned down more jobs than I've accepted. I've just lost my passion for it. Honestly, I'm looking forward to the P-I thing."

A muted buzzing caused Mike to hold up his index finger as he fished his phone out of his pocket. He looked down at the screen with a worried expression. "Excuse me," he said. He pushed a button then held the phone to his ear.

Maggie could tell something was wrong. She watched Mike's eyes move back and forth. Occasionally, he looked at her, but he was not saying much.

"Okay, I'm on my way." Mike stood and shoved his phone back into his pocket. He ran his hand through his hair, leaving it sticking up at a few odd angles.

"Everything okay?" Maggie asked.

"We need to go," he said.

"Okay, no problem." Maggie stood. "Is everything okay?"

Without answering Mike cleared the table of all the remnants of their meal, wadding it all together, even Maggie's half-eaten sandwich. Then he threw it all in the large trash can sitting at the edge of the porch. "It's my sister," Mike finally replied. "Something is going on at work. Do you mind if we stop at my house before I take you back?"

"No problem," Maggie said, "I'm in no rush."

Mike's house was only five minutes away. His sister's car was already parked in the driveway when they pulled up.

"Do you want me to wait here?" Maggie asked.

"No way, come on in, let's see what's going on. Heck, you might be able to help."

"Whatever I can do," Maggie said, but even as she climbed out of Mike Marker's car, she had the uncomfortable feeling she did not know what she was getting herself into.

Mike's sister, Joanie, was waiting by the back door when Mike and Maggie walked around the garage. Joanie was a surprisingly petite woman with shoulder-length brown hair. She was wearing a dark blue suit with a light blue shirt under the jacket. Maggie would have had a hard time imagining Joanie and Mike were related if it hadn't been for their matching bright blue eyes.

Mike unlocked the back door. "What's going on, sis?" he said, motioning the two women inside.

"Who is this?" Joanie said. She pointed to Maggie as if Maggie couldn't hear her rudeness.

"Oh, sorry," Mike said. "This is my friend, Maggie, from Boca."

"I didn't know you had a girlfriend in Boca," Joanie said.

"She's not my girlfriend," Mike said, a little too adamantly.

"*He's* not my boyfriend," Maggie added, just in case it wasn't clear.

Joanie rolled her eyes Then she sat down in one of the kitchen chairs. Mike and Maggie sat across from her, waiting for her to tell them what had happened.

"It's Aunt Millie," she said, tears forming in the corner of her eyes.

"What happened to Aunt Millie?" Mike asked. "Is she okay?"

"She isn't hurt, or anything, but all her money is gone. And it's all my fault." Tears now ran down both her cheeks…"

"What do you mean all her money is gone, and why would it be all your fault?" Mike asked.

Joanie took a deep breath before explaining. "It was almost five o'clock. Aunt Millie came into the bank. I was in my office, closing down for the day. I wasn't paying attention when the clerk came in for my approval. I didn't look at the amount on the check. I just signed it since I knew Aunt Millie was planning on remodeling her master bathroom."

"How much was it for?" Mike asked.

"At first, I thought it was ten thousand dollars, but when my daily receipts were off, I went through the transactions and saw my authorization for a hundred thousand."

"Aunt Millie had a hundred thousand dollars in the bank?" Mike asked, surprised.

"No, Mike," Joanie said, putting both hands on her face. "She had over a million dollars—and it's all gone. Her entire life savings!"

"Why would she have a million dollars in a bank instead of with an investment company?"

"It's that generation," Joanie said. "Honestly, I'm surprised Aunt Millie didn't hide it under a mattress or in a coffee can buried in the back yard."

Mike placed a fist under his chin, his elbow on the table. He took a minute to himself, lost in his thoughts.

Finally, he sat back. "How is it possible? Doesn't the bank have controls in place for this sort of thing?"

"That's the problem, no red flags," Joanie said, wiping her face. "I didn't see the full effect until I closed the books for the day. There was too much variance in the bank's assets. I looked and analyzed everything. My cashier issued ten checks made out in Aunt Millie's name, each for one hundred thousand dollars."

"So now, Aunt Millie has ten cashier's checks for a hundred thousand dollars?" Mike asked.

"No." Joanie narrowed her eyes. "When I called Aunt Millie and told her there might be a problem with her account, she said she already knew. I started to breathe normally until she explained that she was working with a bank examiner."

"So why is that a problem?" Mike asked.

"It's a scam, Michael! There is no bank examiner. Aunt Millie is being scammed. It happens to a lot of older people. Someone poses as an official. The mark, in this case Aunt Millie, believe they are part of an official investigation. They are excited to help."

"Why?"

"I guess it gives them something to talk about with their friends at Bridge Club."

"I guess we better go talk to Aunt Millie," Mike said, looking at his watch.

"We can't go tonight," Joanie said.

"Why not?" Mike asked

"She went to bridge club."

"Well, I guess there isn't anything we can do tonight anyway," Mike said. "Let's meet here at eight tomorrow morning and head over together. I can use some time to work through a plan of action."

Joanie walked out not saying goodbye. Mike and Maggie sat silently listening to her car door slam, and the engine fade into the distance.

Finally, Mike looked at Maggie. "Welcome to Salisbury."

SATURDAY

CHAPTER 2

The Itinerary

Aunt Millie's house was a modest brick home similar to most of the homes in the area. Whitewashed rocking chairs lined up across the wide covered front porch. Large flower baskets hung at both ends. A large tulip tree shaded the driveway, where an older Chevrolet sedan was parked.

"It looks like she has company," Maggie said.

"No, that's her car," Mike said.

"I thought you said your aunt was ninety-two?"

"She is."

"She drives?"

"Yes, she does." Mike smiled. "You'll see."

Joanie pulled in directly behind Mike and appeared next to Mike's car door before he could even get out.

"Before we go in," Joanie said, "I don't think we should tell Aunt Millie the complete story."

"Honestly, I think we should call the FBI and report the scam," Mike said. He and Maggie stepped out of the car.

"What if we…or rather, you…can talk to Aunt Millie and convince her that her money isn't gone, and it's just part of the bank examiner's test."

Mike shook his head. "Lie to our ninety-two-year-old aunt?"

"Please, Mike, can you just look into it before we report it. I'll lose my job. I could go to jail."

"Who all knows what happened?" Maggie asked.

Joanie shot her a sideways glance. "Just me, aunt Millie, the teller, and the phony bank examiner," Joanie said, returning her focus to her brother.

Mike took his flipbook from his front pocket and a pen. "Have you spoken with the teller?"

"I tried to call her last night, her phone was disconnected. I'll text you her address, maybe you two can drive by and talk to her. I'll bet she's in on it somehow."

"What's her name?" Mike asked.

"Tina Turner," Joanie said.

"Seriously?" Mike tilted his head.

"That is her real name," Joanie said.

Mike wrote it down, shaking his head.

"Do you think she was using an alias?" Maggie asked.

"That's an excellent question," Mike said.

"What are you going to do, Mike?" Joanie asked.

"I'll talk to Aunt Millie and let you know," Mike said.

He walked to the front door. He had barely knocked when the door flew open.

"Michael," Aunt Millie said, wrapping her arms around his middle. Mike responded, engulfing the small woman and pulling her to his chest.

"How are you doing, young lady?" he asked, holding her out at arm's length.

The woman didn't look anywhere near ninety-two years old. She wore a pair of fashionable blue jeans and a red short-sleeved Nike shirt. Her Nike shoes were emblazoned with a bright red swish. Her hair was pulled back in a long blonde ponytail. Maggie assumed Aunt Millie's hair was a high-end wig: it was a little too perfect—and a little too blonde—for someone her age. From a distance Aunt Millie could easily pass for someone in her fifties, but when close enough you could see the deep-set wrinkles in her neck and face. Her arms displayed brown age spots, but her golden tan lessened the impact. No matter how old she was, she was a beautiful woman.

"Auntie, this is my friend, Maggie McFarlin."

Mike stepped aside to allow the two women to meet.

"Hi, Maggie," Aunt Millie said. "Nice to meet you."

Maggie held her hand out and received a solid shake. "Nice to meet you."

Millie turned to Joanie. "And how is my beautiful niece today?" The two embraced.

"I didn't sleep well," Joanie said.

"I can tell, dear....Let's all sit down."

Aunt Millie pointed to the chairs. As they all settled in, she disappeared into the house. A short while later she came out with a pitcher of tea and four glasses filled with ice. She handed Maggie a glass. "Where are you from, Maggie?"

"She's from Boca," Mike answered, speaking for Maggie.

"But Seattle is my actual hometown," Maggie said. "I've been in Boca for a few years now."

"Very nice, my dear, how did you two meet?"

"Can we do this later?" Joanie pointed her finger between the two. "Mike?"

"Auntie, we're actually here to talk about the bank examiner. Can you tell us everything that happened from the very beginning?"

Aunt Millie placed the tray on the wicker table between the two chairs before she settled in on the whitewashed swing fastened to the rafters by thick black chains. Maggie and Mike turned their rocking chairs to face her, and Joanie moved from her chair to the seat next to her aunt on the swing. Mike waited for Joanie to settle in before he again took out his small flip notebook.

"It was last week sometime. I received a telephone call from a man who seemed very legitimate."

"Sorry," Mike interrupted, "do you have the number he called you from?"

"I suppose it would be on my phone's history," she said. "I haven't erased anything."

Aunt Millie took her phone out of her back pocket and flipped through a few screens before handing the phone to Mike.

Mike copied the phone number into his pad before giving the phone back to his aunt.

"Okay, great," he said, nodding.

"We met at the park in Granite Quarry. He even brought me a Frappuccino and a chocolate croissant from Starbucks. I have never had a Frappuccino before. It was delicious. Have you had one?"

Mike and Joanie both shook their heads.

"They *are* the best," Maggie offered.

"They sure are," Millie agreed.

"Anyway…" Mike prompted his aunt.

"He told me that he needed my help. He showed me a badge."

"What did the badge say?" Mike asked.

"I didn't read it," Millie said. "I admit, I was a little nervous but excited to be chosen for the investigation. Honestly, Michael, I thought you kids would be impressed."

"Okay, did he give you a name?"

"Mr. Sellers or Stellers, he said he was a bank examiner investigating one of the tellers at Brownstone Savings and Loan. I should have called you"—she looked at Joanie with watery blue eyes—"but he said I shouldn't tell anyone."

"Did he know you were my aunt?" Joanie asked.

"I don't know. I don't think so. The guy gave me an envelope with a withdrawal slip all filled out. He even knew my account number. All I had to do was take it to the new girl, Friday at four forty-five exactly. Which I did yesterday."

"Then what?" Mike asked.

"I took the envelope directly to him where he was waiting at the park in Granite Quarry. I handed it to him, and he gave me five crisp one hundred dollar bills. He called it a convenience fee since the money in my account would not be available until Monday morning."

"Auntie?" Joanie asked, "how much did he 'borrow'?"

"It was ten thousand dollars."

Joanie stared at her aunt. "It wasn't ten thousand dollars,

Auntie. It was a lot more."

"That's not possible," Millie said. "The man was very specific when he explained that it would be ten thousand dollars."

"I'm so sorry." Joanie bent over and began to weep.

"It's okay, sissy." Millie put her hand on Joanie's back.

"It's not okay." Joanie's words were muffled by her hands covering her face.

"Auntie, it seems your account is missing a million dollars," Mike said. Millie froze. Her hand stopped soothing Joanie's back. Finally, she stood and started to sway. Mike stood just in time to catch her before she hit the porch floor.

"Oh my God, call 9-1-1," Joanie said.

Maggie fished out her phone and started to dial.

"I'm okay," Millie said, choking on her words. She sat back on the swing. "Don't call."

Maggie froze, looking to Mike, who shook his head and mouthed, *It's okay.*

Millie looked from Joanie to Mike. "What am I going to do?"

"I don't know what happened, Aunt Millie, but I promise you I intend to find out," Mike said. "I just need a little time to look into it. Can you trust me to do that for you?"

"Of course, whatever you say." Aunt Millie now seemed surprisingly calm. "But I will tell you that I can't survive on my six-hundred-dollar-a-month social security. I am ninety-two years old, and I don't have much time left on this earth...Heck, I don't even buy green bananas anymore. If I don't get that money back, I will have to sell this house...My father, your grandfather, built this house...I was born in this house...." She hung her head, seeming to fight tears, but when she lifted her head, her eyes were dry and void of any emotion. "It is your inheritance."

"We're going to figure this out. I promise, Aunt Millie. You won't have to sell your house," Mike said.

Joanie spoke up. "I have an idea. My branch won this year's customer service award, and the prize is an all-expenses-paid Caribbean cruise. Everyone who had access to the information needed to pull off this scam will be there. The corporate marketing manager was supposed to be on the cruise, but her husband was exposed to COVID. Now they've been quarantined. You can take their place and investigate undercover."

"You just said your corporate marketing manager is a woman. Your coworkers might be suspicious if I show up," Mike said.

Joanie tilted her head toward Maggie. "Your friend could come. You two could be a couple."

"I don't know, Joanie..." Mike said, looking at Maggie, who stood stone-faced.

"I think it's a great idea," Millie said.

"Someone in my bank is a thief, Mike. It had to be an inside job. They knew who to target and how much they could get and how to avoid the flags," Joanie said, tears again forming in her eyes.

"What if the perpetrator isn't one of the people on the cruise?" Maggie asked.

"The so-called bank examiner Millie met with might not be the mastermind of the whole

scheme—but someone who was in on it had to have access, and everyone with access will be on the cruise."

Joanie said, speaking directly to Mike even though Maggie had asked the question.

"Well, Maggie?" Mike turned to her. "Would you like to go on a cruise?"

Maggie sat speechless for a moment. She looked at Mike, back to Joanie, and finally, at Aunt Millie, all eagerly waiting for her to speak.

"I thought you would never ask," Maggie said.

"Great," Mike said, "but if we don't get anywhere by the time we get back, we'll call the FBI."

"Deal," Joanie said, standing again. She wiped the remaining tears from her face with the back of her hand. "I'll send you the itinerary right now." She pulled out her phone, scrolling through her email.

"When is the cruise?" Maggie asked.

Joanie looked up from her phone. "Sunday."

"Next Sunday?" Maggie's eyes opened wide. "Like, seven days from now?"

"Like, tomorrow. Sunday." Joanie tapped some buttons on her phone. "You two need to go see Trevon as soon as possible. I just sent you his contact information."

"Do you have your passport with you?" Mike asked Maggie.

"I do," Maggie said, patting her handbag.

"What am I going to do with Zoey?" Mike asked.

"She can stay at my house with my kids," Joanie said. "They'll be fine, and Aunt Millie is here if they need anything" Joanie's mood suddenly seemed restored with hope.

Millie stood up and held up her glass. "Anyone…more tea?"

Maggie shook her head. She hadn't even touched her first glass, which sat on the side table still full, sweating almost as much as Maggie.

"I think we're going to get some breakfast," Mike said. "Would you two like to join us?"

"Oh no, you kids go on. I have a lot to do around this place," Millie said, "in case I have to sell."

Joanie rolled her eyes. "I'm going to stay here with Aunt Millie," she said the next moment. She stood and leaned over to Mike to whisper: *"I need to make sure she's okay."*

"That's probably a good idea," Mike said in a low tone. "She's acting a little *too* okay." He turned back to Aunt Millie. "Love you, Auntie."

"Goodbye, Michael—and nice meeting you, Maggie. You kids have a good time on the cruise."

Millie waved before walking into her house, balancing the tray loaded with the abandoned glasses of tea.

"I'll be right back, Auntie," Joanie called through the open door. "I need to move my car." Then she turned to Mike and Maggie, motioning them to follow her. "Before you two go, I need to give you something," she told them. She smiled as she walked to her car. She popped the trunk and pulled out a bag, which she handed to Mike. "A little something to wear at the bon voyage party. It's tradition."

Mike accepted the bag and told his sister he would talk to her later that day. He and Maggie walked over to Mike's car. He held the passenger door for Maggie, who slid in.

Finally settled into his seat, he handed Maggie the bag. She set it on the floor in front of her purse.

"I don't think your sister likes me," Maggie said as she fastened her seat belt.

"She's just overprotective. As soon as she gets to know you, you'll be best buddies."

"I don't know about that."

"Breakfast?" Mike asked, backing out of the driveway.

"Please, I'm starved," Maggie said, thinking back to her last meal, a half-eaten chicken sandwich.

CHAPTER 3

Blame It on the Drink Package

"Grits or livermush?" the waitress asked.

"Gross," Maggie said before she could stop herself.

"She's not from here," Mike explained apologetically.

"Well, bless her heart," the waitress said. She shifted onto her other foot, her eyes peering over the glasses that sat on the end of her nose. "What *side* would you like with your eggs, honey?"

"Sorry," Maggie said, "do you have just regular hash browns?"

"Sure do," the waitress said. She turned to Mike. "What about you, darlin'?" She winked.

"Two eggs over easy, ham, and grits."

"Country or city?"

"Country," he said, handing her his menu.

As soon as the waitress walked away, Maggie asked: "What's the difference between country and city ham—but much more important, what the heck is livermush?"

"Country ham is simple, like a country boy. It's dry-cured over a long period of time. City ham is a lot fancier. It's wet-cured in a solution of saltwater and sweet flavors and then smoked using hardwoods for a more smoky flavor. Now liver-mush, I'm pretty sure it has pork liver and secret spices. Honestly, I have no idea what it is, but it's not bad. It's deep-fried so..."

"It must be a Southern thing."

"It's most definitely a Southern thing"—Mike smiled —"specifically, a North Carolina 'Southern' thing." Mike made air quotes with his fingers.

"I have to say... I'm pretty impressed with your knowledge of pork products. I never knew there was a difference in ham. Usually, ham is just ham."

She tucked her menu behind the metal napkin dispenser, as the waitress hadn't bothered collecting it from her. Then she pulled several napkins from the tightly stuffed box and wiped the surface of the table in front of her. The sticky substance she was trying to clean off didn't disappear until she poured some of the water from the well-used plastic water glass that sat in front of her and wiped it down. She inspected the salt and pepper shakers and wiped them down too. Before she put down the salt shaker she noticed that it contained rice for some reason.

Freed from having her arms stick to the table, she leaned back in the booth. Mike smiled and shook his head as he watched her. "You're a long way from Boca."

Maggie smiled. "I am perfectly capable of roughing it."

"Roughing it?" Mike's eyebrows came together.

"Livermush?" Maggie returned his look but smiled wide.

A man wearing blue coveralls and sporting a baseball cap and work boots stopped and looked down at them.

"Well, if it isn't Mike Marker?" the man said.

Mike looked up and smiled. "Hey, Dicky." Mike put his hand out in greeting.

"You back in town?"

"Shur'nuff"—Mike's drawl was suddenly back—"been here for a coupul'a months now."

"I heard about..." Dicky looked between them, noticing Maggie sitting there for the first time. He stopped himself. "Well, sir, I'm sorry for ya loss."

"Ya', thanks, man, 'preciate it."

A few more locals stopped by to greet Mike.

"Is this the first time you've been out and about?" Maggie asked.

"I've been keeping a low profile since I've been back," Mike said.

"That's probably the reason your business is slow. You probably should get out there, join the Chamber of Commerce, and maybe the local Lions Club."

"That's not my style," Mike said just as the waitress set two plates in front of them.

"Anything else I can get y'all? Tabasca?"

"I'm good," Maggie said.

"Me too," Mike said, releasing the waitress to bring coffee to the table behind them.

Maggie looked at her plate, which was overflowing. "That's a lot of food." Mike's ham was thick and took up half his plate.

"How did you sleep last night?" Mike asked, changing the subject from his hometown's cuisine.

"Fine," Maggie said. "It's not the Ritz, but I slept like a rock. I was exhausted from the drive."

"Well, you look great." Mike smiled.

Maggie felt her face heat up. Either she had just blushed at the compliment or had a minor hot flash.

"What I really need is a mimosa," she said, looking for the waitress.

Mike smiled slightly. "They don't serve alcohol here," he said.

"Of course they don't."

Maggie pulled several more napkins from the dispenser. She wiped the top of her water cup then took a drink. She got the waitress's attention and motioned for a cup of coffee.

The waitress set the coffee and a small bowl filled with creamers in front of Maggie but walked away before Maggie could thank her.

"We need to take our documents to the travel agent after breakfast," Mike said. "The guy has to fax it all in before the end of the day to change the tickets."

"No problem, but I also need to find some time to go shopping. I didn't pack my cruise attire. Do you think we'll be doing the formal night?"

"I emailed you the itinerary earlier." He held up his phone. "But I believe there is at least one formal night. We can run over to Concord Mills Outlet Mall and pick some things up after we get the tickets sorted out."

"Okay," Maggie said. Then she remembered she had brought the bag in that Joanie had given them. She picked it up from the foot of her chair and handed it to Mike.

He pulled out two dark blue T-shirts. He handed one to Maggie and held the other against his chest.

"'Blame it on the Drink Package'?" Maggie said, reading the sizeable white print in the middle of the shirt. The words were printed over a cartoonish image of a cruise ship. She unfolded the shirt Mike had passed to her. The words and images were the same. "Clever," she said, "but I'm not wearing this."

"Joanie said the whole group would be wearing them on the first night. It's funny. Plus, you heard Joanie, it's tradition."

"Well, this is an extra-large, I wear large, soooo...."

"Maggie, we have to blend in."

"We can't blend in without wearing matching shirts? How do we know that the person—or persons—who scammed your aunt will even be on this cruise?"

"We don't, but it makes sense that an insider is involved, and most likely it's a manager or someone higher up, all of whom will be on the ship with us."

"How is the bank going to operate with all its key people on a cruise?" Maggie asked.

"I'm sure they'll bring in people from other branches to fill in."

"What if that's all part of the plot?"

"It's not."

"I wish I wasn't the bank person. I don't know anything about banking," Maggie said.

"You should probably do a little internet research tonight; but honestly, all you really need to do is blend in and make friends. Hopefully, someone will say something or do something to expose themselves. Undercover is all about adaptability and thinking on your feet."

"Are you sure no one from your sister's bank will recognize you as Joanie's brother?"

"The only person who might have isn't going. You're taking her place."

"Won't the other people from Corporate expose us?"

"No one else is going from Corporate," he said, "but all good questions, Maggie. I think there's hope for you."

*

The travel agent was already sitting at a large booth with a laptop and mobile scanner when Mike and Maggie arrived at the Starbucks where the agent had set up. Mike motioned to Maggie, indicating she should slide in, but Maggie shook her head, so Mike took the seat.

"Hey man, how's it going?" Trevon said half standing. He held his fist out. Mike bumped Trevon's fist with his fist.

"This is Maggie," Mike said. "Maggie, this is Trevon."

"Nice to meet you, Trevon." Maggie smiled. "I'm going to get coffee. You guys need anything?"

"Nice to meet you too, Maggie, and thanks, I'm good." Trevon pointed to the drink sitting in front of him.

Mike shook his head.

Maggie ordered herself a venti latte with an extra shot and a Teavana Mango Black Tea for Mike, even though he had said he didn't want anything. She slid into the booth next to Mike and set the tea in front of him. She held out her coffee, offering him a taste of her drink.

"No, thanks," he said, "I'm good with the tea."

"You don't know what you're missing," she said.

Then she noticed Mike's passport as Trevon handed it back to him. It had his picture but not his name. She leant closer to him. "Are you using an alias?" she whispered.

"Yes, but my first name is still Mike, so don't worry about it."

"Should I use an alias?"

"Do you have a different passport?"

"No," she said, now digging hers out of her purse and handing it to Trevon.

"Well, then use your real name. Just avoid using your last name, and no one can Google you. But honestly, why would they? Everybody will be focused on having a fun vacation, not on who we are."

Trevon smiled, pretending to ignore their quiet conversation. He continued to spend the next few minutes typing their information into his system. Then he finally sat back on the bench. "All done. I emailed you all your documents. The only thing you need to do now is to check in online as soon as possible. I would suggest you do that even before you leave this spot. Then the only other thing you need to do is print out the luggage tags."

"Thank you for the quick turnaround," Mike said.

"You know I would do anything for your family. We've been friends for a long time." Trevon folded his laptop and placed it into his large satchel along with the scanner. He took a long sip from his straw before sliding out of the booth.

"I hate to rush out of here, but I have another appointment at the library, so y'all have a good time on your cruise and call me if you need anything else."

Mike reached over and exchanged another fist bump with Trevon before he departed. Maggie slipped out of the booth and took the seat across from Mike.

"What's next?" she asked.

"I guess we better go shopping," Mike said.

Maggie hadn't been in a mall for years. She preferred to shop online or at Target, where mothers with baby buggies were less likely to run you down. This mall was quiet but had plenty of brand-name stores. As soon as they walked through the over-sized mall doors, they found themselves at the entrance of the Tommy Bahama store.

"Perfect," Maggie said.

She pulled Mike into the store but released him at the Men's section while she examined the racks of colorful island-themed dresses, loose-fitting cotton shorts, and flowy tops. Soon she had an armful of appropriate cruise apparel, which she piled on top of the sales counter.

"Would you like to try these on?" the sales clerk asked.

"Nope, I'm good."

She looked across the store and spotted Mike. He was holding up a shirt. When he noticed her looking his way, he pointed to the shirt. She gave him two thumbs up. The blue would match the color of his eyes perfectly, she thought.

When the sales clerk completed the transactions, Maggie had two large bags full of clothes.

"Good job, Maggie," Mike said as he came up to the counter. "That was the fastest shopping trip in history...especially with a woman," he added, lowering his voice as if he was speaking to an invisible friend.

"What was that?" Maggie asked, narrowing her eyes but smiling.

"You didn't try anything on," Mike said, placing the shirt he had been looking at on the counter. He handed his credit card to the sales clerk.

"I'll try it all on later at the hotel."

"So, we're set?"

"Almost," Maggie said. "I need something for formal night. I promise not to take too long."

"Not a problem. If you want, I can take all this stuff to the car. I have a few phone calls to make, so I'll wait for you there."

"Perfect."

As she wandered through the mall after Mike returned to the car, Maggie spotted an Anne Klein. She hurried into the store and went straight to the center racks. She picked out three dresses and tried them all on, but in the end she chose the first one she had tried on. It fit her perfectly.

Happy with her purchase, she smiled as she slid into Mike's car. He was talking to some of his clients using the car's

Bluetooth, so Maggie was able to hear both sides of the conversation. It appeared that former Detective Mike Marker did more than find lost dogs, after all. He was conducting research for a defense attorney regarding a domestic issue in Rowan County and searching for a lost relative due an inheritance for a client in Georgia.

When Mike finally disconnected the call, he announced, "Calendar cleared."

"So, you do work for a living...."

"Yeah, I get by. There's one more issue I need to deal with before we go."

"What's that?"

"My daughter."

"Do you want to drop me off at the hotel?" Maggie asked.

Mike smiled. "No, I might need the backup."

No problem, Maggie thought. *I'm great with kids*.

A short while later Mike pulled into his driveway and parked next to Maggie's SUV. He helped her load her purchases into the back of her car.

"Thanks," she said.

Before Maggie could get her driver's side door open, the back door of Mike's house flew open, and an enraged teenage girl appeared, her arms folded angrily across her chest. She quickly approached Mike then stood inches from her father's face.

"I am *not* staying at Aunt Joanie's."

"Yes, you are," Mike said calmly. "You're not old enough to stay by yourself. Plus, we need you to help with Joanie's kids."

Zoey backed off a bit, relaxing her shoulders. "Am I getting paid?"

Mike nodded. "I think we can arrange some compensation."

Zoey smiled. "Okay, but you have to add unlimited data on my phone."

"You can hook up to the internet. You don't need unlimited data."

"Fine, whatever."

Zoey gave up, having already known the answer.

Mike said: "Zoey, I'd like you to meet Maggie McFarlin, from Palm Beach."

Maggie held a hand out. "Hi, Zoey."

Mike's daughter brushed past her and disappeared through the back door.

Mike shrugged his shoulders. "Teenagers."

"I know she's been through a lot with her mom and all. I can understand."

"Unfortunately, she was the same way before her mom died. They are a lot more alike than I wish, but hopefully she'll grow out of it. She's a bright girl, maybe even Ivy League. At least that's the track she's headed on."

"Well, that's awesome," Maggie said.

A loud voice came from behind the screen door: "Dad, there is *nothing* to eat in this house."

"I have to go pack anyway," Maggie said, opening her car door.

"You sure?" Mike said. "I can order in for dinner?"

"No, I'm good. It's been a long day, and it looks like you have your hands full."

Maggie smiled and climbed into her car as Mike held the door.

"Okay, I understand," he said, smiling. "The car will be here at seven tomorrow morning to take us to the airport."

"See you then," Maggie said, waving goodbye as she backed out of the driveway. In truth, she was glad to be leaving the uncomfortable situation.

SUNDAY

CHAPTER 4

Embarkation

At seven o'clock sharp, Maggie arrived at Mike's house with a large, freshly packed suitcase and a smaller carry-on. Most of her traveling clothes had been replaced with the new purchases from the day before. The old garments were now stuffed in grocery bags in the back seat of her car.

The driver of the transport Joanie had hired was out of the vehicle as soon as Maggie pulled up. He took her large suitcase and disappeared at the back of the van. Maggie took the very back seat, careful not to spill the venti latte she had purchased on her way from the hotel.

Mike appeared from the back door, looking fresh. His hair was damp, apparently from his morning shower. He smiled wide as soon as he saw her then took the seat in the back next to her.

"Good morning," he said, fishing out a folded piece of paper and handing it to her.

"Good morning," Maggie said, unfolding the paper.

"Your luggage tags and airline ticket."

Maggie noted the seat number on the ticket. She shook her head then folded the ticket in half and stuck it in her pocket. The van door opened again, and Joanie climbed in. She took the window seat directly in front of Mike, leaving the two center seats and the front passenger seat free.

She turned to face Maggie and Mike. "Before we pick up the rest of the group, let me give you a little bit of a rundown,"

Joanie said.

Mike took his small spiral flipbook out of his front pocket, ready to take notes.

"John Haas is the head of security. He's been with the bank for over fifteen years and at my branch for the last five. Bank security is his second career. He was military police or special forces...something like that.

"What branch?" Mike asked.

"Marines, maybe? I'm not sure, but honestly, what does it matter?"

"It matters to a marine. If you remember, I was a military police officer in the marines," Mike said, narrowing his eyes.

"Seriously, Michael, I don't know his military service history. Maybe you can figure it out. You're the detective."

"Okay, Joanie," Mike said, shaking his head. "Please continue."

"David Sanchez is our I-T guy—and honestly, he's a technological genius. He came to us right out of college and has been with the bank for over ten years. David splits his time between all the branches in Rowan County but works from home most of the time. He only comes in when we need to install new equipment or a specific problem at the office.

"I'm surprised he gets to go on the cruise," Maggie said.

"He had the highest internal customer service scores. I thought it was a great idea."

"Do you think he could be a suspect?" Maggie asked.

"I don't know. As the only technology guy, he certainly has access, the ability to pull it off...*and* he was at the branch on Friday when Aunt Millie came in."

"Why was he there that day?" Mike asked.

"He was setting up the security protocols for the new teller."

"Interesting. Who else?" Mike asked as he was making notes.

"Kimberly Carson is our head teller and has only been with the company for six months. She was working at one of the big banks in town that closed their storefront. Like a lot of the other big banks, they're now only doing business online. Kimberly was the one who hired the new teller.

"Our clientele are mostly local people," Joanie continued. "Like our family, they've been here for generations. They are old school and want to come into the branch to do their business face to face. They don't trust their money in cyberspace. Which is why we won the cruise. Not only did we beat our revenue growth goals, we did it with the highest customer service scores of any of our branches. We scored a ten out of ten. The branch in Faith only has an eight out of ten."

"So how long have you been at the bank, Joanie?" Maggie asked.

"Twenty-one years. I started working as a nighttime janitor while I went to Catawba College. As soon as I graduated, I worked as a teller at one of the branches, was promoted to head of marketing at Corporate, and finally became the branch manager in Salisbury five years ago."

"She's worked very hard to get to this point," Mike said proudly of his little sister.

"It's been a challenge, but I've loved every bit of it. This is the first time I've been worried about my job. I feel helpless. I feel responsible. We have to figure this out not only for Aunt Millie's sake but for the bank's sake—and my reputation."

The van slowed as the driver turned into the bank parking lot.

"That's David and Kimberly, over there." Joanie pointed to the far corner, where two people stood outside their cars, waiting next to their bags.

The driver pulled up and quickly loaded the bags. Kimberly and David took their seats in front of Joanie.

"Where's John?" Joanie asked.

"I didn't realize I was in charge of John," Kimberly said, not bothering to turn around. David just shrugged his shoulders.

"Can we just give it a few minutes?" Joanie called up to the driver. He nodded his head.

"Kimberly, David…this is Mike and Maggie," Joanie announced.

Kimberly didn't turn but waved behind her head.

David turned around. "Hey, guys."

Joanie typed a text and called John, leaving a message. Fifteen minutes later, with no response to either, she instructed the driver to go ahead and take them to the airport.

As soon as they arrived at Charlotte International, Maggie headed for the customer service desk. Mike looked confused but waited for Maggie as the rest of the group checked in using the kiosks. Maggie soon came back and handed him a ticket.

"Here," she smiled.

He looked down. "I don't understand?"

"I upgraded us."

"It's only a two-and-a-half-hour flight, Maggie."

"Let's go to the first class lounge," she said, holding up the thin boarding pass.

"We don't have time." Mike pointed to the large black screen that displayed departures, "We board in twenty minutes."

"Hey guys," Joanie said, "John's still not here."

"Maybe he took the money and ran," Maggie said in a low tone that only Mike and Joanie could hear.

"I honestly don't think so, but, strangely, he hasn't even texted me."

"He *is* your head of security, right?" Mike asked.

"Yes, he is. I tried calling him several times, but it keeps going to voicemail."

"You said he used to be a marine, right?"

"Yeah…?" She looked at Mike, confused; then her face changed in realization. "Awe, now I get it…Improvise. Adapt. Overcome."

"So you do remember, little sister," Mike said.

"How can I forget when you take every opportunity to remind me." Mike attempted to put his hand on her head, but she swatted it away before she stomped off.

"You marines do stick together," Maggie said.

"Once a marine, always a marine."

Mike smiled wide, melting Maggie until she shook it off.

"Let's go, we have a plane to catch," he said. "There's nothing we can do now. If he doesn't show up, we fly without him."

As soon as they were in their seats, Maggie had a glass of wine in her hand, and Mike was thumbing through the seat pocket magazine.

Maggie pointed across the aisle. "Remember those seats?" she asked, taking a sip of her wine.

"Of course I do," Mike said, smiling. "I traded seats to sit next to you flying from Fort Lauderdale to Charlotte."

"I was going to Seattle, and you were visiting your daughter. It seems like such a long time ago. Was you being on that flight truly just a coincidence, or were you investigating me?"

"It was a coincidence, but a good detective never passes up a chance to interrogate a subject. Put that in your private eye toolbox."

Maggie sat up straight. "Was I a suspect?"

"Not really, but your friends were."

"Really? Good thing they were innocent."

Mike cocked his head and raised an eyebrow. "Yeah, I'm still not so sure about that."

"So, how is Zoey this morning?" Maggie asked, changing the subject.

"Doing pretty good. I think she likes hanging out with her cousins. She's a good kid, but as I said, her attitude could use some improvement. I'm trying to be an understanding father... I've cut her a lot of slack since her mom died. I'm not sure if I told you about the accident. It wasn't her mother's fault, but her blood alcohol level was above the legal limit, so that became an issue, and it was printed in the papers. You know how kids at school are, she's had to endure some unwarranted ridicule."

"Poor girl," Maggie said, "Those teenage years are tough. I wouldn't go back."

"My sister has been a huge help. Zoey tells her everything."

"Do you miss being a detective in Palm Beach?"

"Sometimes. But I'm happy to be close to my family, Aunt Millie, my sister, and my daughter."

"It seems like such a small town, not much to do." Maggie handed her now empty glass to the flight attendant, who was preparing the first-class cabin for takeoff.

"Living in a town where people don't lock their doors is a blessing. That's why this financial scam is such a big deal. It just doesn't happen. If people find out about it, Joanie's bank will be in ruins, and my aunt will be devastated."

"Well, I hope we can help," Maggie said.

Just then the plane took off, pushing her to the back of her seat. She closed her eyes until she felt released from the upward thrust and then the sinking feeling.

"That was the flaps retracting," Mike said.

"What are you talking about?"

"The sinking feeling. When the flaps retract, it feels like you're sinking…right before the plane accelerates."

"There seems to be a lot I don't know about you, Mike Marker."

"Well, I know nothing about you, Maggie McFarlin. Every time I ask something personal, you change the subject."

"I need another drink," Maggie said, ignoring Mike as he waved to the flight attendant, who had just unbuckled herself from the jump seat. The flight attendant nodded her head in understanding.

"See what I mean?" Mike asked. But he was speaking to the back of Maggie's head.

Maggie was glad Mike had wanted the window seat. She felt more comfortable with an easy escape, even if it was just the forward bathroom.

*

The plane soon landed at the familiar airport in Fort Lauderdale. It struck Maggie that she was so close to her home in Boca, and it didn't bother her that she wouldn't be going home but heading to a cruise ship.

Mike and Maggie were the first to disembark from the plane. Once they had made their way to the baggage carousel, Mike pointed to a man holding a placard that read *BS*. "Our driver," he said.

"'BS'?" Maggie looked at Mike as he led them over to the waiting man.

"Brownstone Savings and Loan," he said over his shoulder. "They forgot the -L part."

"Of course they did," Maggie said under her breath.

One by one, the group gathered near the baggage area. Maggie moved near Joanie, "Did John show?" she asked quietly.

"He did not, but I did get a voicemail while we were on the plane. He said he drove down yesterday. I guess he has family in the area. It would have been nice if he told me ahead of time. But it's a relief he'll be on board the ship."

When the final piece of luggage was pulled off the conveyer belt and piled on the cart, the group marched to the awaiting Sprinter van. Loading the bags into the back of the van took longer than the drive to Port Everglades Terminal, where the *Silence of the Seas* stood proud, awaiting its upcoming voyage. A long line of passengers waited to enter the terminal building.

The driver unloaded the bags and passed them to a porter...who gave them to another group of porters...who loaded them onto several carts. The driver then pointed to a side door; Joanie handed him an envelope.

Joanie waved to the small group, indicating they should follow her. The bank had sprung for first-class treatment: they stood in front of a side door marked *VIP Guests Only.* A young woman sporting a neat white uniform greeted them and motioned them into the large metal building. The terminal looked like a warehouse. Ropes and luggage were spread throughout. Lines of passengers waited to be checked in. Other passengers sat in plastic chairs, awaiting their chance to board. Mike and

Maggie's small group was led through a path of dark purple velvet ropes, eventually leading to a sectioned off area where a separate sitting area had been set up with oversized furniture resting on a large sectional carpet. The sitting area was still in full view of the other passengers. A small table had been set up with coffee and tea service. Mike noticed a pile of pastries by the tea and eagerly picked off the top offering, an apple fritter.

The young woman in uniform began speaking. "Good afternoon, my name is Mora. It's my pleasure to be your embarkation hostess. Please help yourselves and relax a few moments while I check you in. I will need your identification to process your boarding documents."

The young woman walked around the sitting area, collecting passports; then she disappeared behind a long desk across the room.

"Still no John?" Mike asked his sister between bites.

Joanie looked at her phone and scrolled through a few screens. "John is already on board," she said. "He said he would meet us at the room."

Kimberly approached Maggie. "So you're our corporate marketing guru," she said. . She pulled up her curly long red hair and expertly twisted it atop her head, fastening it in place with some type of plastic claw.

"Yes," Maggie said nervously.

"I liked the Christmas Trees for Kids festival the bank put together last year. You did a great job," Kimberly said.

"I can't take credit for that," Maggie said. "I have an amazing staff."

"I thought the marketing department was a one-man show—or rather a one-woman show," Kimberly said, confused.

Sensing trouble, Mike spoke up. "Hey. David, so you're the genius everyone raves about, technologically speaking of course."

"It's been my passion since I was a kid," David said. "I think I was coding before I could even read."

Before Kimberly could continue to question Maggie,

Mora reappeared. She passed each of them their passports and a thick blue lanyard with the letters *VIP* repeated numerous times down both sides. Attached to the bottom of the lanyard was a clear pouch and a platinum-colored card with each person's name printed across the bottom. Maggie slipped the lanyard over her head, careful to turn the pouch so the card with her name faced inward.

"If you all will follow me, we can get you started on your vacation."

Mora turned, and like baby ducks, Maggie and the rest of the group followed the leader past the long lines of waiting passengers, who simply stared with either envy or disgust.

Mora led them to a gangway separate from where the main crowd was boarding. The ship's crew was also using this gangway to board. Maggie held her VIP pass for the security team's scanner to read. When the light turned green, a member of the security team directed her to a red X painted on the deck. She smiled as the computer recorded her photograph. Then she stepped aside as each member of the group followed her in turn.

"Why do we need to be photographed?" Kimberly asked as she stepped up to the red X.

"In case you fall overboard, they can identify the body," David said.

"Hilarious, David. Maybe you should volunteer for comedy night."

"We have very tight security aboard the *Silence of the Seas*," Mora said. She held the elevator door for the group. Then, when they were all in, she pushed the button for Deck 11.

CHAPTER 5

Muster Stations

When the elevator doors opened, the group exited to what looked like the lobby of a penthouse in a fancy New York apartment building. The carpet was a vibrant deep blue with white swirls resembling ocean waves, the walls were painted in the same hues, and the door jams and fixtures were highly polished brass, creating a nautical theme. The window of a large porthole filled the space with natural light and a dynamic view that Maggie knew would change with the landscape of their voyage. The island sounds of a steel drum echoed from somewhere in the corridor, welcoming them to their weeklong residence.

Mora pointed to a large gold door with a plaque that read *Private.* "This is the private club reserved for our VIP guests and private affairs." She pointed to the VIP plastic sleeve hanging by David's chest. ""These will allow you entry into the club as well as into your room. You'll use the card for everything: ordering drinks at the pool, shopping in the plaza, or gambling in the casino."

She then moved to the door located directly across from the private club. The door also held a plaque with large letters spelling *OASIS.* She pulled a thick platinum card from her front pocket and waved it close to the raised pad above the handle. The door latch *clicked,* and she opened the door. The group filed in and assembled in the middle of the room.

"Nice," Maggie said in Mike's ear.

"Welcome to the Oasis." Mora smiled. "Our most exclusive suite on the *Silence of the Seas*." She held her arm out; Maggie and the rest of the group filed past as they explored the suite. There was a large professional kitchen and a generous group living space with a big-screen television. A fully stocked bar sat between the two.

"Are we still on the ship?" David asked.

A voice behind Maggie said, "Welcome to the *Silence of the Seas* and your own personal oasis." Maggie turned. Standing at attention were two men; one, a large red-faced man in a white coat and a chef's hat, the other a much shorter, darker-skinned man with his hair slicked back.

"Please let me introduce your chef, Chef Paul, and your steward, Ralph," Mora said, smiling.

"May I start you off with a drink?" Ralph pointed to an ice bucket. "I have champagne chilled, or"—he pointed to the bar —"anything else you require."

"I'll have a glass of champagne," Maggie said.

The other members of the group followed her lead.

"Please, enjoy the balcony," Ralph said. He slid the giant glass doors aside, allowing the group to file out to the expansive private balcony. "I will bring the drinks out shortly."

"Wow," Mike said, stepping out onto the balcony, "this is awesome."

He pointed to the six-person hot tub. Maggie took a seat on one of the six lounge chairs that sat in a long row facing the ocean.

"There's another fully stocked bar out here," David said, taking a seat at a café table.

Kimberly leant against the rail, her eyes staring toward the horizon. "This is the bluest water I've ever seen."

"Wait until we get into the Caribbean," David said.

Maggie focused on the familiar Florida water before closing her eyes, remembering the first day she arrived in South Florida from Seattle. The feel of the sun heating her skin and breathing in the thick salty air...It was like breathing in a whole new life.

"This is something, huh?" Mike said, sitting next to her.

Just then Ralph delivered their drinks. Maggie opened her eyes and sat up. Mike took two of the crystal flutes from the tray Ralph held forward. He handed one to Maggie. "Cheers," he said.

"Cheers," Maggie repeated, taking a small sip of the clear bubbly liquid.

"Your bags have arrived, and I put them in your room if you would like to change," Ralph told the group.

"Perfect," Mike said. He stood and held a hand out to Maggie. Ralph finished passing the drinks to the others before he slid the giant glass doors aside again and motioned for them to follow.

Ralph opened one of the doors and motioned to the pair. "Your room."

Mike and Maggie stood frozen. Both their bags sat near the bed.

"Whose room is this?" Maggie asked.

Ralph looked concerned. "Both?"

After an awkward pause, a voice spoke softly behind them. "Remember, you two are together." It was Joanie. "I'm bunking with Kimberly, and David and John are sharing, so..."

Maggie felt her cheeks turning red. "Tell me there is another room."

"I'm afraid not," Ralph said behind them. "But I can pull the bed apart into two singles. Not a problem."

Maggie took a long sip of her drink, emptying the glass.

"Is that a problem, Maggie?" Mike smiled slyly.

"Nope. No problem," she said. *Except my snoring.*

"Good, problem solved," Joanie announced as she walked away.

"I can sleep out here on the pull out if you would rather me..." Mike offered.

"Don't worry about it," Maggie said nervously, "we'll make it work."

"That's the spirit." Mike walked into the room and looked

around. "Look, there's a private balcony." He pulled back the long curtains.

"How wonderful," Maggie said, wishing her glass was full again.

A loud unfamiliar voice shook them from their dilemma and lured them back into the main living space. A very tall, bald gentleman dressed in cargo shorts and a Tommy Bahama shirt stood next to Joanie and David.

"You must be John," Mike said, taking a few steps toward the man holding his hand forward.

"I am—and you are…?" John asked, looking at Joanie, confused.

"Aw, this is Mike and Maggie. Maggie is the corporate rep for the trip."

"Well, nice to meet you." He nodded to them then tilted his head up and looked around. "I had no idea there were rooms like this on a cruise ship."

"Let's get you a drink, John."

Joanie led John over to the bar. Maggie followed, filling her glass with the remaining champagne. Chef Paul set out a cheese tray. Noticing the empty champagne bottle, he pulled a new bottle from the wine refrigerator, unscrewed the wire loop on the cage, then, draping a towel over the bottle, carefully popped the cork. He pushed the bottle into the ice bucket. Then he handed John a tall glass filled with a light pink concoction.

"You're rooming with David," Joanie told John.

John lowered his eyebrows. "We have to share?"

"Seriously, John," Joanie said. "We could have booked interior staterooms. Count your blessings."

"Don't worry, John, I don't snore," David offered.

"Well, I do," John said proudly. "My ex-wife says I sound like a freight train traveling through Grand Central."

"I'll put my earbuds in." David smiled.

A disembodied voice came from the speakers somewhere above them: *Please make your way to your muster stations.*

"Everyone must participate in this exercise," Ralph announced to the group. "You have time to finish up your drinks before we go. I'm happy to lead you to your muster station, if you like."

The group took their time finishing drinks and using the bathroom even as Ralph grew noticeably impatient.

"We really must go," he said, "they will take attendance. The ship cannot sail until everyone has mustered."

"Why didn't you say so," John said, emptying his glass and setting it down. "Let's go.

*

The Brownstone Savings and Loan group were the last to show at Muster Station 4B, which turned out to be quite fortunate. They suffered a few side glances from other passengers who had been waiting for almost twenty minutes in the crowded breezeway, but they were fortunate to assemble at the very edge of a large crowd that was at least seven deep. The assembled groups spanned the entire outside deck; there wasn't much space between them and the other muster stations. Their position would allow them to be the first to leave. Only a few more stragglers showed, and they were positioned at the front again, keeping their group on edge.

"I just want you to know I can be a little agoraphobic," Maggie whispered to Mike.

"What do you mean a *little* agoraphobic? You are agoraphobic, or you're not."

"I sometimes have panic attacks when I'm in large crowds."

"Are you alright now?" Mike asked in a way Maggie felt was a bit insincere.

"Yeah, as long as we stay at the edge and I can get out of here before they start pushing me." Maggie took a deep breath and tried to push away images of the crowd coming at her when they were released.

"I remember a guy in my unit in the marines who ended up in a loony bin because he was locked in a box," John said. He was standing on the other side Maggie.

"That's horrible." She turned her attention more fully to John. "Why was he locked in a box in the first place?"

"It was a training exercise for special ops," John said. "Apparently he had some kind of disorder the doctors failed to pick up on during the psych exam."

"That sounds like claustrophobia, but it often results in symptoms similar to a panic attack," Mike said.

"You're well versed in more than just pork products," Maggie said.

"It was part of my job," Mike said in a low tone.

"I think a lot of it is mental," John said, pointing to his head.

"I agree that it is mental, and most of the time, I can breathe through it," Maggie said, "but sometimes I just lose control and start shaking, my hands get clammy, my heart races, and I feel dizzy. One time, I was at Disney with some friends, and they convinced me to go with them to the nighttime parade. I agreed and was okay until the parade ended—then an entire park full of people were all exiting at the same time through the same gates. I tried to just go with the flow, but the crowd was thick, surrounding me, pushing and touching until I lost it and fainted. I was lucky the crowd didn't trample me. Two young women pushing strollers created a barrier until the paramedics reached me and revived me with smelling salts. It was pretty embarrassing."

Mike looked worried. "Has that ever happened again?"

"There was college graduation, Saturday's at Costco, and..."

"Well. Let's not take a chance. As soon as they wrap this thing up, you get out of here. I'll meet you in the room"

"It's all about breathing," John offered. "Keep your head out of the crowd and concentrate on your goal."

"What's my goal?"

"Would you three be quiet?" Kimberly had turned and was looking directly at Maggie. "I'm trying to listen in case there is a real emergency."

"Sorry about that," Mike whispered.

Kimberly turned back toward the ship's crew as they demonstrated the proper donning of a life jacket.

Maggie didn't even pretend to pay attention to the instructions. She had been on a few cruises and knew the drill; so as the crew wore their cruise-ship smiles while reciting the importance of safety on board the ship, Maggie looked to her left, where another group was receiving the same information. A moment later, the disembodied voice from the loudspeaker announced: *In case there is a real emergency, and that emergency requires the evacuation of the ship, this is the spot where you will board your lifeboat.*

Maggie looked at the bright yellow boat hanging from the side of the ship in front of them, and then she considered the crowd standing around her. There was not enough space on that boat for all of the passengers. She decided not to worry about it, because the likelihood of an event requiring everyone to abandon ship was almost infinitesimal.

The ship wasn't the *Titanic*, and even if it was, Maggie knew that out here in the Caribbean, there were usually two or three cruise ships practically in sight of each other—and she could swim. She decided she would rather face a few hungry sharks than get on that boat with all of her fellow passengers.

She again turned toward the group to her left. She noted the sliding glass door between the two groups. She would head straight for the door as soon as possible.

She had a solid plan, and she took a deep breath, letting it out slowly. Just as she was about to turn back toward the sea, she noticed one of the passengers in the group assembled on the other side of the door: was he waving to her? She waited a moment.

Then the passenger waved again—and it was *definitely* meant for her. She shook her head and squeezed her eyes shut, but when she slowly reopened them, she saw him. Silas. Waving at her.

Maggie turned to her group; all of them were distracted.

So she motioned a small wave back. Then she realized who was standing right next to Silas.

Jay.

What the heck are these guys doing on this cruise ship? she asked herself.

The last time she had seen these two was when they climbed aboard a private jet after rescuing her from the trunk of a murderer's car. She had never told Mike Marker about Silas or Jay because she didn't know how to explain the whole relationship, and she needed to protect her friend Alex from further suspicion. It was complicated. But now, how was she going to keep her identity secret from the group? She smiled to Silas and motioned to the door. Silas nodded his head in understanding.

"This thing is almost over, and I have to go to the bathroom," Maggie told Mike, leaning into him. "I'll meet up with you later."

"Are you sure you're okay?"

"Absolutely."

She smiled tightly then moved slowly to the bulkhead. She slid down, dipping out of sight, just as the groups were released. When Mike turned back, Maggie had already disappeared through the large sliding doors into the ship.

CHAPTER 6

Atrium

Maggie rushed through the breezeway and hurried to the center of the ship, where she stopped in amazement. She was in the ship's atrium. Four grand staircases—one on each side—curved gracefully down from three decks above. Each staircase was decorated by intricate golden banners. The staircases lead to a central floor, as stunning as a ballroom in a castle. A chandelier of Chihuly glass hung above the center. A grand piano stood at one end, and two classic Rolls Royce cruisers were parked on the opposite side. The cars seemed to be guarding the entrance to Kensington Gardens: the London park had been authentically reproduced just behind the cars.

Maggie spotted Silas and Jay coming through the passageway. They were followed by the masses, who were already starting to enter the space. She made her way to the park entrance and motioned for Silas and Jay to follow her.

She walked quickly until she reached a small alcove off the main path. She found two park benches facing each other near the center of the faux park. Silas and Jay casually walked down the path and sat on the park bench directly in front of the bench where Maggie sat.

Maggie's face was red. She was breathing hard from both the panic caused by the crowd and the shock of seeing Jay and Silas on the ship.

"No offense, Maggie, but I think you need to hit the gym," Silas said.

"Seriously?" She looked at the two. "What the hell are you guys doing on this ship?"

"A little R-and-R, of course," Jay said.

"Did Alex send you?" Maggie asked. Alexandra was one of Maggie's best friends at Banyan Tree Country Club. She was a fierce businesswoman and once known as the Mistress of the Mob.

"Why would you think that?" Silas said with a wink. "What if I just missed you?"

"Because I called both Alex and Britney last night and told them I was coming on this cruise to investigate something, and you two just happen to show up." Britney was Maggie's other best friend at Banyan Tree Country Club.

"What are you investigating?" Jay asked.

"It's a bank thing, and I happen to be undercover," she said proudly.

"I noticed you're with that detective," Silas said with a smirk. "But I'm pretty sure it was me who pulled you out of that trunk last time you and your buddies decided to investigate something."

"I thank you for that, but really, this isn't dangerous, so I won't be requiring your services. Feel free to enjoy your vacation."

"Even though we aren't your body guards, *this time*, and since we will be onboard anyway, feel free to call on us if you need us to save your butt again." Silas put on that Cheshire cat smile of his.

"Don't worry, we'll stay out of your way," Jay said.

"Unless you want something in your way," Silas said.

Maggie blushed. She remembered a few steamy nights with this handsome Latin Casanova. Even though he had been on the job, she had enjoyed herself; but now was a different time, and she hadn't figured out her feelings for Mike.

"Just know we have your back. If you need anything, we're in cabin 8-2-2-0," Silas said, standing.

Maggie nodded her head.

"By the way, Maggie"—Jay tilted his head toward her—"do you happen to have the notebook with you?"

"What notebook?" she asked, attempting to hide her shock.

"The notebook from Marco's. Someone took it from his home the night you three ladies were there."

"I don't have any idea what you are talking about." But she knew precisely where the notebook was. Britney took it. She saw her put it under her shirt at Marco's and again when she handed it over to her uncle.

"Okay, no problem," Jay said with a wry smile, He was standing now directly in front of her.

Silas stood and moved between the two. "I'll be in touch," he said, moving Jay aside. He held out his hand to Maggie, who accepted the help to her feet.

The two men walked away, leaving Maggie standing in the center of the path. Silas looked back and waved just before he and Jay disappeared around the corner.

Maggie let out her breath. She hadn't even realized she had been holding it. She knew Alex could be a useful resource to get in touch with, because she knew more about the banking industry than most accountants. Alex might look like a retired kindergarten teacher—she was barely five feet tall—but they didn't call her Mistress to the Mob for nothing. She had a particular influence that extended beyond the borders of the United States.

Maggie pulled her phone out of her back pocket and dialed Britney's number, but her call went directly to voice mail. The ship was still relatively close to the port in Fort Lauderdale, so she should have a signal.

She tried several more times before finally leaving a voice mail. "Hey Brit, this is Maggie. You'll never guess who showed up on this ship—Silas and Jay. I have no idea why they are here or why Alex would have sent them. The weird thing is that they were asking if I had a notebook from Marco's house. Call me as soon as you get this message."

Maggie hung up then called Alex.

Alex picked up on the first ring. "Hey girl, what's going on? I thought you were solving mysteries on a cruise ship."

"I am," Maggie said, "but I was wondering why you sent Silas and Jay?"

"What do you mean?"

"It's not that I don't appreciate it, but I doubt very much I'm in any danger," Maggie said.

"What are you saying?" Alex sounded confused.

"Silas and Jay are on the ship."

"*What?*" Alex's voice increased in volume.

"You didn't send them?" Maggie was worried.

"What did they say?" Alex asked in her business voice. "Exactly."

Maggie considered how much to tell Alex. "They asked if I had some notebook."

"What notebook?"

"I'm not sure. Jay said he thought one of us took it from Marco's desk. I didn't know what they were talking about." Maggie was feeling a little guilty, not telling Alex that she knew Britney had it. "Do you know what they are talking about?"

"No," Alex said.

Alex's answer caused Maggie to doubt her friend, but she was glad she hadn't exposed Britney.

"Has the ship left the dock?" Alex asked.

"Yes."

"Okay, I'll call you back."

Alex hung up, not even saying goodbye.

Maggie thought for a moment. Did her friend not know the guys were on board?. Could they be doing a little freelancing without Alex's knowledge...or was Alex hiding something?

Maggie jumped as her phone vibrated in her hand. She looked at the screen, expecting to see it was Alex calling back, but it was Britney.

"So what the heck is going on, woman?" Britney said without any worry in her voice.

"Did you listen to my message?" Maggie asked.

"That's why I'm calling you back," Britney said. "Don't worry about anything. There is nothing in the notebook that's worth hurting someone over."

"What do you mean 'hurting someone'?" Maggie's voice had risen an octave.

"Did you talk to Alex?"

"I just got off the phone with her?"

"Did you say anything about the notebook?".

"I didn't because I wasn't sure if I should."

"Yeah, please don't say anything. I'm meeting with Alex tomorrow, and I'll bring it to her. But I need to explain some things before I hand it over. And Maggie..." Britney paused so long Maggie thought she might have lost the connection. "Don't say anything to Silas and Jay. Stay away from them if at all possible."

"O-kaaaay," Maggie said, drawing the word out. "Do I need to know something you're not telling me?"

"Of course not," Brittney said. "I'm just shocked they are there. Just keep playing the dumb blonde."

Maggie took offense. "I wasn't playing the dumb blonde."

"You know what I mean," Britney said playfully. "I'll text you later. Love you, have fun with Mikey."

"Bye," Maggie said. She rolled her eyes as she hung up. She put her phone in her back pocket before starting down the path leading out of the park. Just as she rounded the first bend, she practically ran into Mike.

"Hey," she said nervously.

"I was worried and came looking for you."

Was it Maggie's imagination, or was Mike trying too hard not to give away the fact that he had been standing there for a long while?

"Well, you found me," Maggie said.

"Last minute calls?" Mike said with a tilt of his head.

"I was just checking in with Alex and Britney before we set out to sea."

"You three stick together."

"It's that country club where we live. We're three misfits who found each other, and yeah, we stick together."

"If there were anything I needed to know, you would tell me...right, Maggie?"

"Of course," Maggie said, crossing her fingers in her mind. "We're partners."

"Exactly." Mike smiled. "We're partners-and partners don't lie to each other."

Maggie swallowed hard.

"Or keep important information from each other," he added.

"Agree," Maggie said. *But who determines what is important?*

"This park is unbelievable," Mike said, looking around. He reached out and touched a tree.

"It's all real," Maggie said, thankful for a new subject. "Even the grass. You could get a blanket and have a picnic."

"These ships just amaze me," Mike replied. "Did you see there's a full-size waterslide, a professional rock wall, and an ice skating ring?"

Maggie smiled. "All lost on me, I'm afraid."

As soon as they reached the end of the path, they stepped back into reality, transported from an idyllic park setting into the magic of the atrium.

"Do you think someone in our group took your aunt's money?" Maggie asked as they walked through the atrium's center. She stopped and looked up.

"I honestly don't know," Mike said. He followed Maggie's gaze. "Wow!"

"Yeah," Maggie said, amazed at the painted ceiling.

"It's the *Raising of Lazarus* by Domenico Tintoretto," Mike said confidently.

"Do you seriously know that?" Maggie asked.

"It happens that I love art almost as much as you enjoy wine. The original painting is hanging in Raleigh at the North

Carolina Museum of Art."

"Well, I'm again impressed, Mike Marker," Maggie said.

"I think we are getting underway," he said. "Let's go change for the reception."

"Perfect."

Maggie looked around for any trace of Silas and Jay. She considered telling Mike about the two men but felt like it wasn't the right time. How could she spoil the magic that seemed hidden around every corner of the *Silence of the Seas*?

CHAPTER 7

Bon Voyage Reception

Six identical blue shirts arrived at the reception line together. The slogan *Blame It On The Drink Package* inspired a few chuckles along the way. Maggie rolled her eyes. She looked around the room at some of the other groups' matching shirts: *Benjamin Family Reunion* in bright yellow, *Terry's 50'th Birthday* in fluorescent green, and the *Bride* and all her *Bride's Maids* in fuchsia pink.

It could be worse, Maggie thought.

Captain Dillard was a tall blonde Nordic type with a broad smile and straight nose. Maggie imagined his ancestors were the captains of the great Viking ships conquering the world and somehow planted his DNA.

"Velcome to the ship," Captain Dillard said, greeting each guest with a smile and a solid handshake. When it was Maggie's turn, she smiled and noticed the captain wore no wedding ring...*and* he was about the right age. If her friends, Britney and Alex, were with her, she might have had the courage to say something flirty; instead she moved awkwardly down the line to meet the next crew representative.

Jules Gilbert was the cruise director. She took Maggie's hand in both of hers. "Welcome aboard *Silence of the Seas.*" She looked between Mike and Maggie as she took Mike's hand.

A slightly taller but thinner man stood next to her. "May I introduce my assistant Santos. If either of you has any questions regarding fun activities to do while you are a guest, please feel free to ask either of us."

"Thank you both." Maggie smiled at the handsome six-foot man.

"So, what are your passions, Ms. Maggie?" Santos asked with a robust Caribbean accent. His brown eyes were soft but intense. The way he stood looking at her was as if he could see into her soul.

A candlelight dinner, a nice bottle of wine, and a long walk on the beach, Maggie thought to herself. Noticing the faraway look in her eyes, Santos started rattling off a few activities available on board the ship: "We offer rock climbing, surfing, zip-lining, or how about volleyball?"

Maggie narrowed her eyes. "Seriously, do I look like I would enjoy anything that physical. I'm more of a Bingo player," she said.

"Aw, now I see…you like to use your mind and not your muscles," Santos said, winking. "We have a fabulous slot tournament, you can win ten thousand dollars and a free cruise—and, of course, we do have Bingo for your enjoyment. Please let me know if you have any questions this week. I will be available to you." He nodded as she walked away, feeling her face turn hot. As she headed toward the small bar—obviously a temporary setup for the event—she heard Mike discussing the volleyball tournament. *Jules,* she thought, smiling to herself.

"What are you smiling about?"

Joanie walked up to the bar with Maggie.

"Jules is the cruise director," Maggie said. Joanie tilted her head and shook it slightly. "Julie, from *Love Boat,*" Maggie explained, smiling. She turned to the bartender. "I'll take Merlot."

"You're showing your age," Joanie said. "I'll also take the Merlot," she told the bartender.

The bartender set the two glasses of wine in front of the ladies. "Nice shirts." He smiled broadly.

"Clever, isn't it?" Maggie smiled at Joanie as they took their glasses and walked to an empty seating area. Maggie sat on the couch, and Joanie took the overstuffed chair next to her.

They each took a sip of their wine before setting their glass on a long table in front of them. The room, designed for quiet conversation and relaxation, was decorated with over-stuffed furniture, heavy curtains, and thick plush carpet.

"Speaking of *Love Boat...*" Joanie said. She pointed to Kimberly and David, who were sitting at a two-person high top in the back corner of the room. Their faces were close to one another, as if they were sharing intimate secrets.

"Do you think they have something going on?"

"I'm not sure," Joanie said. "I honestly never really notice them interact that much at the bank. Whenever David was at the branch, he was under a desk or in the room with the servers. Kimberly was always busy at one of the teller stations or in her office with a client."

"Do you think this is a new thing?"

"I don't know." Joanie shook her head and again lifted her glass of wine. "It seems a little fishy."

Maggie noticed John sitting at a table set up with staff to sign up excursions. He had several pamphlets in his hand.

Mike took a seat next to Maggie on the couch.

"I signed up for the volleyball tournament with Jules," Mike said.

"Julie?" Maggie smiled.

"Julie, the cruise director from *Love Boat*," Mike said, smiling.

"*If* Julie was a petite black woman from Nigeria..." Maggie added, remembering the country listed on her nametag.

"You two are showing your age," Joanie said.

"I don't know, Joanie, we might actually be on the *Love Boat*," Mike said, tilting his head toward the side of the room where David and Kimberly sat.

"That's what I said." Joanie shook her head, "I think we need to take a look at those two. Together they could have easily executed the scheme."

"Or they are just *really* good friends," Maggie said, also tilting her head. She watched as David gently put his hand on

Kimberly's knee. Kimberly looked across the room. She spotted Maggie looking at her. Maggie quickly turned to Mike, but not before she suffered a narrow-eyed glance from Kimberly.

"Hey Mike, fancy seeing you here!"

A tall, imposing man dressed in a ship's officer's uniform sat himself down in the empty chair across from Mike.

Mike reached his hand out. "Randolph," he acknowledged.

The man took Mike's hand and pulled Mike to his feet. He delivered a testosterone-induced man hug across the table. The next moment he noticed Maggie and Joanie sitting at the table. "Jeez, Mike, you don't seem like the cruise type."

"Actually, I'm on the job," Mike said, nervously looking around. He located John still standing at the excursion table, and Kim and David at the high top. It seemed like none of them had witnessed the exchanges of familiarity between himself and Randolph.

Randolph noted the action and nodded in understanding.

"More importantly, what the heck are *you* doing here?" Mike pointed to the ship's uniform.

"I retired from Palm Beach a few months after you left, but I knew I couldn't stay home and watch the boob tube all day, so I took the job as head of security on this ship."

"How do you like it?" Mike asked.

"I love it. How about you? What are you doing these days?"

"I have a little P-I thing going on in North Carolina," Mike said. Again he looked around, making sure they were still out of earshot of the rest of the group.

"That's right, man, I heard what happened. I'm so sorry about your ex-wife. How is Zoey doing?"

"She's doing okay, typical teenage girl."

"Yikes," Randolph said. He took a seat next to Mike.

"Hey, Randolph, if you don't mind, can we keep our relationship and my background on the down-low. I'm looking into something, and I'm undercover."

"Mike, I don't like the sound of that. Remember, this is my

job here. I'll tell you what, you come to see me in the morning and you can fill me in on the details. If I can help, I will, but if it's something too—"

Mike interrupted him. "I promise you it's nothing but information-gathering. I'll be happy to fill you in tomorrow morning."

"Okay. So now I need to know, who are these two beautiful ladies?" Randolph pointed to Maggie and Joanie.

"This is Maggie. She's assisting me with the case. And this is my sister Joanie."

Mike nodded, smiling to the women.

"Maggie, Joanie," Mike said, "this is Detective Randolph Edwards."

"*Former* detective," Randolph said, staring a little too hard at Maggie. "You look so familiar..." He put his fist to his chin until a big smile appeared. "You're one of those ladies from the country club who showed up for your interrogation at the station in a limo.

Maggie nodded. "My friend Britney rented the limo so we could do happy hour afterward, but yeah, that's me." She looked at Mike, narrowing her eyes. "Was that an interrogation?"

Randolph looked more confused. He moved his finger back and forth, from Mike to Maggie. . "You two together?"

"No!" they said in unison, a little too loudly.

"Just friends," Mike said in a calm voice.

"Unbelievable," Joanie said, rolling her eyes.

Randolph then turned his attention to Joanie. "I've heard a lot about you," he said, smiling.

"I'd rather hear your stories about my brother, if you don't mind," Joanie replied.

"We've had some real adventures. I can tell you that," Randolph said.

"Really?" Maggie raised her eyebrows.

Joanie leaned forward. "Please share."

Randolph turned back to Mike. "Remember that time you were dating that young girl? I forget her name. Jenna or something like that?"

"Yeah, something like that," Mike said, "but maybe we can share stories later."

"Oh no, keep going," Joanie urged.

Randolph turned to her. "I was on a call in Delray, right near Jenna's place. I was pretty sure Mike said she was out of town. Mike and I were even going to meet for a beer later that afternoon, so I called Mike. 'I thought your girl was out of town,' I said.

'What do you mean? She is supposed to be at Ocean Isle with her mother,' he said. 'Her car is in her driveway along with an older pickup.' He didn't even let me finish. He hung up. He stopped and picked up a couple of egg biscuits and showed up at her house. He had a key, so he went right on in. I'm not sure why he stopped for the egg biscuits. Why did you?" he asked Mike.

"I don't know, I think it was just an excuse to stop by. Honestly? I wasn't thinking too clear at that point," he said. "I stood at the closed bedroom door for a few minutes. I could hear the shower running, but when it stopped, I pushed the door open and walked in. Jenna was just walking out of the bathroom, wrapped in a towel. There was a guy in his whitey-tightys sitting on the end of her bed...obviously, they must have just been finishing up whatever they were doing.

"I could have just shot a gig and left, but I had two biscuits in my hand, so I threw them both across the room at the guy, missing on purpose."

"Can you believe he wasted a perfectly good biscuit?" Mike said.

"Why did you miss on purpose?" Joanie asked.

"If I would have hit the guy in the eye and damaged a retina or something, he could have filed a complaint. It would have been determined to be an assault since I'm an officer of the law, not a good career move."

"Let's back up a bit," Maggie said. "What's a gig?"

"Shooting the bird, you know, flipping them off with the middle finger," Mike said as if she should know.

"Never heard of it, must be another Southern thing."

Maggie sat back. She noticed David and Kimberly were heading back to their table. Mike also noticed.

"Hey Randolph, if you don't mind, we'll come by your office and fill you in on what we're investigating," Mike said tilting his head towards the door.

"Absolutely," he stood. "It was nice meeting you folks. Have a safe and memorable trip. Randolph stood, and Mike followed suit.

"I'll be right back," Mike said to the girls.

He followed Randolph to the entrance. He disappeared for a few minutes; when he reappeared he sat back down next to Maggie.

"Who was that guy?" Kimberly asked as she took the seat he had vacated earlier.

"Head of security," Mike said, looking around to avoid more questions.

"He was sure sitting here for a long time," Kimberly said.

Just then John walked up.

"There are some pretty fun excursions," John said, but Kimberly stayed focused on Mike before finally giving up. "You guys need to hurry up and sign up before all the good stuff is full," John continued.

"Great idea." Joanie stood. "I'll go take care of excursions if you all trust me."

"I'll go with you." David looked up from his phone. He had been looking at it ever since he and Kimberly had approached the table.

"Anybody want to go to the casino after this?" John asked the group.

"I'm in," Maggie said.

"Me too," Mike said.

John put his hand behind his ear. "I can already hear the blackjack table calling me...."

"We should be in international waters any minute, so we can head down now if you all want," Mike suggested. "I'm going to hit the craps table."

"I'll meet you down there," Joanie said. She turned and motioned to David. Together they walked over to sign everyone up for a selection of exciting excursions.

"I want to change," Maggie said. She pulled at the bottom of her shirt.

Mike smiled. "You don't like the shirts?"

"It's not that I don't like them…" Maggie began.

"I *love* my shirt," John said.

"I think it's hilarious," Mike added.

"Of course you do," Maggie said, "but I'm going to change and meet you guys in the casino."

"Do you want me to go with you?" Mike asked.

"No, I'm good. You go see what you can do at the craps table."

*

Maggie made her way up the elevator. When the doors opened on Deck 11, she jumped in surprise. Randolph stood just outside the elevator, waiting to get on.

"Funny meeting you here," he said, smiling wide.

She smiled, holding the door for him. "Yeah, what a coincidence."

"See you tomorrow," he said as the door closed.

She used her key card to unlock the door to the suite. Ralph was arranging the decorative pillows on the couch.

"What was Randolph doing here?" Maggie asked.

"Who do you mean?" Ralph sounded confused.

"Wasn't the head of the ship's security just here?"

"Not that I'm aware of," Ralph said.

He turned his back to her and disappeared into the kitchen. "Do you need a drink?" he called from around the corner.

"No, thank you."

Maggie turned, confused, and went into her room. Her suitcase was sitting on a luggage holder near the bed closest to the wall. Ralph had separated the large bed into two separate twin beds and moved a side table between the two. She dug through her clothes and pulled out one of the new shirts she had purchased. She put the T-shirt she was wearing into the trash bin.

62

CHAPTER 8

Casino

The casino was alive with activity. All the card tables were occupied, except for two or three chairs at the higher stakes tables. Maggie walked through the labyrinth of slot machines, which whistled, rang, and *beeped* different musical octaves as she passed. She spotted Mike by the roulette table. John had already settled in at the craps table.

Maggie began to sneeze when a woman blew cigarette smoke toward her.

"Bless you."

It was Joanie's voice directly behind her.

"Thank you," Maggie said. She sneezed again "It's the cigarette smoke."

"Yeah, since this is the only indoor smoking area, it gets pretty thick," Joanie said. "Let's go over here"—she pointed —"the air scrubbers will kick in soon."

Mike looked over and spotted Maggie. She pointed out where Joanie suggested they move, and he nodded.

Maggie sneezed again as she followed Joanie to a space near the cashiers' cages. Jules, the cruise director, was sitting at a low table, a laptop set neatly in front of her.

"Hey ladies."

Jules smiled wide, exposing a mouth full of beautiful straight white teeth. Maggie had always been envious of people with perfect teeth. She had spent so much money trying to perfect her own, but nothing was good enough. She had spent *thousands*. Now she wished for the small gap between her front teeth.

"Hi Jules," Joanie said.

"You ladies want to sign up for the slot tournament?" Jules asked. "The grand prize is ten thousand dollars, and we have lots of other prizes, including five thousand for second place and a free cruise for the top five places."

Maggie smiled and turned to Joanie. "I don't know..."

Joanie's face lit up. "I think we should do it!"

Maggie raised her eyebrow. "Okay, I guess...What do we have to do?"

"It's twenty dollars to enter, but you get twenty dollars free play in the casino, so if you were going to gamble, it's basically free. The first round starts Tuesday. All I need is your sea cards."

Maggie lifted her lanyard over her head and handed it to Jules. Jules took it and typed the info into the computer. As soon as Jules handed it back, Joanie passed hers across the table.

"Hey, ladies." David and Kimberly were suddenly standing behind them. "Why aren't you gambling?"

"We're signing up for the slot tournament," Maggie said.

"I want to do that." Kimberly abruptly elbowed past David.

"You just give her your card." Maggie pointed to the card hanging from her lanyard. She had already placed it back around her neck.

"Are you going to do it?" Kimberly asked David.

"I think I'll let you girls have all the fun. I'm not much of a gambler," David said.

"You don't have to do anything but push a button," Joanie said.

"I'm going to skip it this time," David said as Kimberly handed over her sail card to Jules.

Joanie put her lanyard back over her head. "You're missing out," she said. "I'm going to see what I can do with my twenty-dollar credit in the *Wheel of Fortune* machine over there.

She walked away, leaving Maggie with David and Kimberly.

"This is going to be such fun," Kimberly said, taking her card back.

"Remember to be here about ten minutes before two to get familiar with the rules and a practice round. We start right at two. Good luck, ladies," Jules said.

"Thank you," Kimberly replied. She turned her back on Maggie and grabbed David's arm. "David, come help me figure out the machines."

Maggie looked toward the craps table. John now stood at the head of the table. Mike was standing to the side, bent over, placing chips at various spots on the layout.

Maggie ordered a glass of wine from one of the servers roaming around balancing small trays in one hand and taking drink orders. The servers' multitasking ensured the gamblers had no reason to leave their machines or betting tables. The smoke had dissipated as the smoking woman had moved to a different slot machine and the air handler was doing its job. Maggie stood behind Mike and peered over toward John.

Trays of colored chips rested in front of each player. A man holding a long flexible stick was manipulating the dice around the table while two others, one on each side, were busy collecting the losing bets and distributing the winnings. It all seemed to move so fast. Maggie was having a hard time understanding the basics.

"How do these people keep track of everything that's going on?" she said aloud. She did, not expect an answer, but a tall gentleman standing next to her decided he would be her craps encyclopedia. He started talking about pass lines, shooters, boxcars, and Michael Jordan.

His explanations just confused her further. Maggie smiled and shook her head, feigning understanding while tuning his voice out. Her wine finally showed up. She decided to go ahead and order another because she knew one wouldn't be enough.

Mike finally noticed Maggie behind him. He reached back

for her. She moved next to him, filling the spot vacated by a frustrated gambler.

"How are you doing?" Mike asked.

"Great, how about you?" She pointed to his half-full tray of light green chips.

"I'm about even, but John, over there, is killing it. He rolled a seven on his first roll and has hit big on the table."

Maggie recalled something the tall man had said. "I thought seven was bad," she said, surprised that she had actually been paying attention.

"It's good if it's the first roll. I'm surprised you didn't hear the cheers when it happened."

"I was busy signing up for the slots tournament," she said. "Plus the noise from all these machines is a little overwhelming."

"Sweet, another old Mike."

Mike smiled as the dealers piled a stack of chips in front of him. He reached down and stacked them sideways in the tray in front of his, leaving his original bet in place.

" 'Another old Mike'?" Maggie asked.

"A four and a five, Michael Jordan's number," Mike said.

"It looks like John is doing pretty good."

Maggie pointed to four piles of chips being pushed John's way as the stickman delivered the dice back to his hands. The players around the table were stacking chips all across the layout. The action once again became a frenzy, making Maggie dizzy. Mike set a few chips at three locations.

"I'll bet there's more than twenty thousand dollars in chips in front of him," Mike said.

"What?"

"He started with a pretty big stack in the beginning. I saw a bunch of hundreds come out of his pocket. He laid it out there like it was nothing. Seemed a little bold for a security guard."

"It does seem like a lot of cash for a security guard, even if he is the head of security."

"With an ex-wife," Mike added just as John rolled again.

"I'm going to get out of here," Maggie said. "I'm feeling a little claustrophobic."

"And up pops the devil!" Mike said as both dealers swept all the chips toward them, leaving a clean board. The players were quiet as the dealers started restacking the colored chips.

"What happened?" Maggie asked.

"He rolled a seven." He bent over now, placing more chips across the board.

Maggie rolled her eyes. "I'll see you later. Keep an eye on the suspect."

She turned to leave. She was met by a server, who traded her empty wine glass for a full one. She looked around and saw Joanie at a machine watching the wolves and princesses pop up, and lines zigzagging across the screen.

Maggie continued weaving through the slot machines, making her way toward the exit, when she spotted Kimberly sitting at a progressive slot machine. David was leaning over her. Maggie peered over as she walked by. It looked like Kimberly had $125 in credits.

As soon as Maggie walked out, the noise level faded. The further she got, the more the noise faded, and the more relief she felt. Finally, the weight on her shoulders lifted; she could breathe normally. She hadn't realized how stressful that place was—the people, the noise, the smoke. She walked until she reached the wine bar and found a quiet seat in the corner.

Here she could keep away from the noisy crowds and enjoy the Spanish guitar music being strummed out by a young musician with long bangs. He sat on a small platform in the corner opposite Maggie's seat. She noticed a young couple sitting at a bar and several older women seated near the small stage.

The server came over, and Maggie ordered a California Pinot Noir. She rarely drank something so light, but she was trying to be spontaneous.

As soon as the server brought the wine, she became disappointed in her choice. She apologized to the server, and ordered a Cabernet. While she waited for her wine, she pulled her phone out of her back pocket and turned it on. She had set it to airplane mode to avoid letting it roam, but she had turned it off until they were far enough offshore to connect to the ship's Wi-Fi. She found the ship's network and entered her last name and cabin number. A pop-up window indicated she was connected.

She flipped through her Facebook account once the messages started popping in. She tapped her messaging icon, and found several messages from Britney and a phone message from Alex. She was about to listen to Alex's voice mail when a dark figure appeared and took a seat across from her.

Silas.

"What are you doing here?" she asked.

"I'm on a cruise. I'm having a drink," he said, sitting back comfortably.

The server showed up and placed Maggie's wine in front of her.

"I'll have a Bud Light," Silas said before the server even asked.

"We have Miller Lite and Corona Light," she said, smiling.

"Is it icy cold?"

"Yes, it's in a refrigeration unit," she said, a little confused.

"Bring me a glass of ice," Silas said, "just in case."

"You got it, sir, anything you need," the server said as she walked away.

"So?" Maggie asked.

"So what?" Silas asked back.

"What are you doing here? I talked to Alex, and she seemed surprised that you and Jay are on this cruise. Don't you work for her?"

"Aw, yes. Well, Alex is one of many clients," Silas said, smiling as his beer showed up. He took his time pouring the beer in the glass of ice.

"That's just weird," Maggie said as she watched. He ignored her comment but instead ordered another beer.

"It's never cold enough, and I'm going to drink it before the ice melts, so it works."

"Are you on a job for someone other than Alex?" Maggie asked. "And why were you asking me about a notebook?"

"Look, Maggie, I like you. You're smart, funny, and beautiful...but I have to work. I don't have a retirement plan, or I might be able to bring something to the table," he said, looking at her. He reached for her hand. She wanted to pull it away but decided to see where this was going.

"What are you saying?"

"We had a lot of fun, you know. I actually can see us as a couple." He was looking into her eyes, and she was resisting every instinct to pull away. She shut her eyes tightly then opened them slowly, making sure she wasn't dreaming.

"Okay," was the only thing she could conjure, still trying to see where Silas was going.

"We're not getting any younger, and I would love to settle down."

"Okay," she said again, unable to think of anything else to say. It was the server who broke in, setting down an ice bucket full of ice and several beers.

"That's what I'm talking about

Silas smiled and fished a hundred dollar bill out of his pocket then handed it to her as a tip.

"I'll bring your change," she said.

"No change. It's all yours."

"Oh, thank you, sir, thank you, thank you," she repeated, staring at the bill in her hand.

"That was generous," Maggie said.

She released her hand from Silas' and she took a sip of her wine.

"So where were we?" Silas said.

"You were going to tell me why you are on this ship and what I have to do with it."

"No, that's not it." Silas shook his head. "I wanted to tell you that if you want to be together, I need at least two hundred and fifty thousand dollars."

"What?" Maggie blinked several times, replaying his

words.

"If you want me to quit my job and travel with you, I need some kind of assurance."

"Okay, I am *so* confused right now," she started. "Are you saying you would like to date me and be my travel companion, but you would want me to give you a quarter of a million dollars to do so? Is that what you're saying?"

"It sounds bad when you say it like that. I'm just saying that you are getting to the age where it's harder to find someone, and we like each other. We were very compatible, if you know what I mean."

"Oh my God, Silas." Maggie's voice rose, and she stood.

"Shhh!" he said, motioning her to sit back down.

She sat but continued in a loud whisper: "I am only fifty-six years old. I don't need to pay someone to sleep with me or be my traveling companion. There are plenty of apps for that."

"Maggie, you're taking this all wrong. I said you are beautiful, smart, and I like hanging out with you."

"I don't even know who you are or what exactly you do. I just had a weak moment, and Britney talked me into dating you for a minute. I can't believe you approached me like this. I don't even know what to say. I..." Maggie stopped. Her heart was about to explode. She felt a lump working its way up to her throat. She gulped it down as she stood again, tears welling at the edges of her eyes. She turned her back to Silas as she walked out, hearing his last words: *"You'll never find another guy like me..."*

The words stung. The loneliness of her life, served on a silver platter. Silas was a nut case, but he wasn't wrong. She had no choices, but it wasn't because she hadn't tried. Still, he was right. The dates she had ventured out on were awful. Dating was harder when you were in your fifties. She couldn't hold it in any longer: she let the tears roll down her cheeks. She found a restroom and ducked into one of the stalls, where she sat on the toilet and covered her face with her hands. That was when she remembered the messages waiting for her on her phone.

She stood to fish the phone out of her back pocket when it slipped and fell into the toilet.

Oh no! she told herself as she quickly fished it out. She knew not to turn it back on. *What else can go wrong?* she asked herself as she opened the stall door—and almost ran right into Kimberly.

Kimberly looked Maggie from head to foot. "What's wrong with you?"

"I dropped my phone in the toilet."

"Gross."

Kimberly continued past Maggie and entered the next stall.

Maggie went to the sink and splashed cold water in her face. With a paper towel she blotted the mascara that had melted down her face.

Soon Kimberly came out and washed her hands next to Maggie.

"You okay?"

Kimberly glanced at Maggie's reflection in the mirror. She seemed to be genuinely concerned.

"Yeah, I'm fine, just tired," Maggie said, actually feeling the exhaustion in her limbs.

"I'm heading up if you want to walk with me," Kimberly said.

"Sure." Maggie attempted a smile but couldn't.

The two women silently walked to the elevator. Kimberly took the lead. Just before the doors opened at Deck 11, Kimberly said, "Whatever it is, it will be okay."

Maggie didn't respond. She couldn't help see Kimberly in a new light. Maybe her rough exterior was a cover for a much more compassionate person. As they entered their suite, Kimberly asked Maggie for her phone. Maggie handed it to her without question; she would have analyzed it more, but it had been a long day. She walked in a zombie state straight to her bed, where she pulled the covers over her head and fell asleep before another tear could fall.

MONDAY

CHAPTER 9

Purser's Office

When Maggie woke up the next morning, her head had cleared. She was full of determination instead of her pity party from the night before. She found her phone in a bag of rice sitting on the nightstand beside her bed. She picked it up and rolled it around on the blankets before opening it and pulling it out. Kimberly must have somehow found rice and put it in the bag for. The only thing she remembered before going to bed was handing Kimberly the phone.

She found the charger and plugged it in, hoping the rice had done its job and that the dip in the porcelain pond hadn't done permanent damage.

"Well, good morning, sleepyhead."

Mike walked into the room, holding a cup of coffee, which he kindly held out to her.

"You are a saint," she said, eagerly accepting the cup of heaven. She took a sip, closing her eyes, feeling the hot liquid travel from her lips down her throat, to the place deep inside her where coffee did its magic. She took another few sips before opening her eyes again.

Unfortunately, Mike was still standing in front of her with judgment in his eyes. He was holding two small pills in his open palm as an additional offering.

"Aww, no thanks," she said, "I'm a professional. I don't get headaches."

"You look professional." Mike looked at her fully clothed

body. "Maybe just keep them in your pocket in case."

She took the small pink pills from his palm and set them on the dresser behind her.

"Thanks."

"Can you be ready in—"

"Half hour," she answered before Mike had a chance to say *ten minutes*. It was evident that he had already showered. The smell of soap and aftershave was strong, and his hair, what he had of it, was combed back. A tiny bit of shaving cream foam remained on his left ear, where he had missed. She wanted to wipe it off for him, but it seemed too intimate of a gesture.

"Okay, so get out so I can get ready," she said, backing him out the door and shutting it behind him. She set her back to the door, took a deep breath, then headed for the shower. On the way, she picked up the two ibuprofen Mike had given her and swallowed them down with her coffee, just in case.

On the way out the door, Maggie picked up the ship's daily planner, called "The Daily Must Do's."

"Here's something fun," she said as they rode the elevator down to Deck 4.

"Joanie scheduled us for the jeep tour in Cozumel."

"We're already in Cozumel?"

"Look at the top of that planner. It says 'Welcome to Cozumel.'"

"Oh, whoops."

They walked around, trying to find the security office, where they expected to meet Randolph. But they spotted him sitting in the purser's office. He was leaning back in a swivel chair, eyes closed, feet up on his desk, his hands folded across his chest.

"I think he's asleep," Maggie whispered.

"Randy!" Mike shouted.

Randolph jumped, almost falling out of the chair.

"Jeez, Mike. You scared the you-know-what out of me."

Mike smiled wide. "Sorry."

"You *look* sorry."

Randolph stood to greet the two with a handshake from across the desk. "Please sit." He motioned to the two chairs facing him.

"Why are you sitting in the purser's office?" Mike asked.

"Well, I'm temporarily doing double duty. I'm the purser and the security chief. As you see, things are a little slow right now. Our ship's actual purser is on emergency leave."

"Oh no," Maggie said.

"Oh, it's not bad, it's a good emergency. His wife just had twins."

Mike raised his eyebrow. "Sounds like he has his hands full."

"Uh, you could say that. Her two little bambinos are number six and number seven. Now I ask you, how does a guy keep having so many kids being on the ship six months at a time?"

"I think you just answered your own question," Maggie said as she took a seat. Mike followed suit then inched his chair closer to the desk.

"So, Randy," Mike started, attempting to change the subject, "we wanted to come down here and fill you in with what's going on."

"Yes, please."

Randolph pulled his chair in and picked up a pen.

Mike started right in. "My sister uncovered a scheme at her bank to defraud elderly people. The scammer poses as a bank examiner who asks an older person to withdraw a specific amount of money. In this case, the phony bank examiner asked for ten grand but ended up with over a million. He couldn't have done it without the help of someone on the inside. Fortunately, all the employees who had the knowledge to pull off the operation—and the opportunity to do it—happen to be on this cruise."

"It seems like a strange coincidence, don't you think?" Randy asked. His pen was poised but he didn't write anything down.

"Well, it happens that her particular bank was recognized

by Corporate as the top bank in North Carolina in customer service, so they treated the top ranks with this trip, all expenses paid."

"They didn't spare any expense, I gather. You're staying in the best suite on the ship."

"It may not be someone on the ship who is the mastermind," Maggie said, letting both Mike and Randy know she was fully engaged in the investigation. "But they would at least need the assistance of one—or, for that matter, several—of the bank associates."

"So why doesn't she just call the authorities?" Randolph asked, flipping his pen between two fingers.

"Because the victim, in this case, is my aunt Millie, who is ninety-two years old. They stole her entire life savings. As you know, in these cases the money is rarely recovered. Unless the person has the money in their possession, it's lost. Even if the culprit is apprehended, they might serve five years, and there's never a guarantee they would ever be able to pay restitution; meanwhile, my aunt is destitute."

Randolph leaned back in his chair, putting the pen in his mouth. "I guess that makes sense." He considered the facts Mike had just told him. "So you believe that one of these bank people is responsible for taking your aunt's money...or that they can lead you to who did?"

"Exactly," Mike said.

"But there's still no guarantee you'll be able to recover the money. Let's say you figure it out. The person is just going to admit to the scheme and give it all back?" Randolph said with the pen still in his mouth.

"I'm not saying it's the best plan, but it's the only opportunity we have at the moment."

"Who are you most interested in?"

Randolph now seemed ready to write. Maggie noticed all the pens in the cup sitting on the purser's desk had chewed ends.

"There are three people from the bank here on the cruise, all of whom had access and opportunity; one of them has to know something, but I'm not sure about motive. We have David Sanchez, the I-T guy, Kimberly Carson, the head teller, and John Haas, the head of security."

"What about the bank manager? He isn't a suspect?"

"The bank manager is my sister, Joanie, and she's the one who brought this to us. She just wants to get our aunt's money back and save her job."

"You know she is going to lose her job when the company finds out she didn't go through the proper protocol with this matter?"

"I think the best outcome would be if we find out who did it and get the money back before having to report it to the Federal Trade Commission—if, at that point, it would even be necessary to report it to the authorities."

"The F-T-C doesn't resolve the complaints anyway," Maggie said. "Just more red tape before the matter is actually investigated; and as far as motive, that's easy. Money."

"That's true." Mike nodded in agreement. "Money is the best motive in the world. But do you think someone who just stole almost a million dollars would come on this cruise? Why not? A million bucks isn't going to be enough to hide on a tropical island. Maybe ten million."

"You know, your aunt may not be the only one who has been taken in by this guy," Randolph said. "A lot of these older people either don't notice or are too afraid to say anything when they realize they've been scammed, in fear of losing their independence. Your problem might be much bigger than just your aunt."

"You're right, but my concern, or rather our concern"—he pointed back and forth, between Maggie and himself—"is to resolve Aunt Millie's money."

"No, I completely understand, so whatever help you need, let me know," Randolph said.

"Well, there *is* something you could do for us," Mike said.

"What's that?"

"Can we have access to the security tapes that show some

of the activities of the members of our group?"

"That's fine," Randolph said, "but you would have to know where they were. The ship has a lot of security cameras, and they are constantly recording. Unless there's an incident, the video tapes over itself every forty-eight hours. I don't have the staff to review all the tapes. There is no way I have the staff to sift through them. Also, there's no audio, so I'm not sure anything we see will help."

Mike's face turned down with disappointment.

"But I'll have my people keep a close eye out and let me know if they see anything suspicious. Speaking of suspicious..." Randolph's serious expression dissolved into a smile as he leaned forward in his chair. "Tell me how this all happened." He pointed back and forth between Mike and Maggie.

Maggie felt her face turn hot.

"There isn't anything to tell," Mike said. "After the murder in Boca was solved, we just kept in touch. Ms. McFarlin is studying to become a private investigator, so I took her under my wing. She agreed to help me out on this case."

"I'll bet she did." Randolph winked at Maggie.

"True story," Mike said. He stood and held his hand out to Randolph, who accepted the gesture. Maggie also stood.

"Well, thank you for the heads-up anyway," Randolph said.

"You're welcome," Mike said. "Sure looks like a sweet deal you got here, Randolph."

"It's not a bad gig, for sure. Collecting retirement pay from Palm Beach and free travel to exotic places. It's better than sitting at home in front of the boob tube watching reruns of *Gunsmoke* or *Wheel of Fortune*."

"I don't see you a stay-at-home kind of guy."

Mike held the door for Maggie, but before she walked through it, she turned to face Randolph. "Where were you coming from when I saw you at the elevator on Deck 11 last night?"

Randolph shuffled a few folders on his desk. "I was just checking things out," he said.

"Were you in our room?"

"I walked through," he said.

"Did you see Ralph?"

"He was there, why do you ask?"

Maggie smiled. "No reason, just wondering."

"What was that all about?" Mike asked as they headed down the passageway.

"I'm not sure," she said, "but after I saw Randolph in the hall, I asked Ralph if he had seen Randolph, and he said no."

"Maybe he didn't," Mike said.

"Of course he did. How could he not have? Every time we come in the suite, he comes out to greet us. When I walked in, he was straightening up the living room. It's just weird."

"Honestly, I don't think anything nefarious is going on, but I can ask him later."

"Don't bother. You're probably right; it's nothing. So what's next?" Maggie asked as they walked back into the section of Deck 4 she called Main Street. Shops lined both sides of a wide promenade for almost the entire length of the ship. Most of the passengers were heading toward the gangway.

"What time is our excursion?"

Maggie looked at her watch. "We have less than an hour to meet out on the pier."

"Do you need anything from the room?"

"I have everything I need right here." Maggie leaned toward him; a small backpack hung from her shoulder. "But, I could use a coffee." She pointed to a café across Main Street. "They have pastries."

"I'm in." Mike licked his lips and rubbed his mid-section as they headed for the café.

They sat at the '50s-style café table, Maggie with a venti vanilla latte and Mike with a Mountain Dew and two bear claws.

"You never talk about your family," Mike said as he took a big bite of one of the bear claws.

"Not a subject I enjoy very much," Maggie said.

"Have you been married before, your parents alive, any

kids?" Mike asked Maggie as he took another bite.

"I have a sister in Silverdale. It's in Washington State. You know where that is, right?"

"Sure, remember I was stationed at the submarine base when I was in the Marines." Mike sat up straight as if he was still a Marine.

"That's right. You did tell me that. You know, I actually worked there too." Maggie said taking a sip of her coffee, "right out of high school."

"I don't think you ever told me that." Mike sat forward, "I thought you said that you were a technical writer for Boeing?"

"I actually did both. Working at the shipyard is how I put myself through college."

"That's incredible." Mike said, "what did you do?"

"I was an electrician," Maggie said narrowing her eyes to match Mike's questioning look.

'That's just too cool, Maggie, really. I'm impressed."

"It's really not that big of a thing Mike but thanks."

"My sister's husband still works there. He is the head of Logistics," Maggie said.

"Did you grow up in Bremerton or Silverdale?" Mike asked.

"I grew up in Tacoma."

"Is that where your parents live?" he asked.

"My parents both died a long time ago."

"I'm sorry." Mike reached for Maggie's hand but she pulled back. There was nothing worse than a man feeling sorry for her.

"...And my ex-husband still lives there." She added for effect.

"Why did you leave the Pacific Northwest?" Mike ignored her last comment.

Maggie looked at her watch. "We better get going. The group will be waiting."

"You're a mystery, Maggie McFarlin."

Maggie just smiled as she slung her backpack over one shoulder.

CHARISSE PEELER

"I try."

CHAPTER 10

The sign at the pier said *Welcome to Cozumel.* As soon as they stepped off the gangway, they were encouraged to pose for pictures with members of the crew who were dressed in native garb. Tables had been set up to check out a beach towel or buy a bottle of water for the day. Booths hocking the cruise line's wares—sunglasses, carved coconuts, T-shirts—lined both sides of the pier. If Maggie had a need for a tchotchke, there were unlimited opportunities.

At the end of the pier stood a large tent with several people holding small signs indicating the ship-approved excursion. Maggie pulled the tickets from her backpack and handed them to Mike.

"Hey guys. Over here."

Joanie appeared, signaling for them to follow her.

Mike and Maggie followed Joanie through the crowd. The other passengers were busy dividing into groups, gathering around the multitude of signs for various excursions. When all of the Brownstone group was present, the woman holding the sign that said *Jeep Tour* signaled them to follow her.

"My name is Camilla," the excursion organizer said. "Please follow me to the best jeep tour on the island." She walked briskly to a dirt parking lot a few blocks from the pier. Several flatbed trucks converted to transport the ship's passengers were awaiting them.

"This will be an experience you will never forget," Camilla said. Maggie laughed. Camilla was repeating word for word the words printed on the brochure. Her final words were lost as she released the group to two young men standing at the ready.

"Welcome, all," one of the men announced. "Please, find a seat."

A short ladder leaned against the rear of the truck. The tour guide assisted Maggie as she climbed up the ladder first. At the top she was met by the second young man, who held his hand out to help her maintain her balance.

Maggie took a seat on one of the crude wooden benches closest to the front. It looked like the safest place to sit. Joanie came up next and took a seat next to Maggie, probably figuring the same thing. Kimberly took the position on the other side of Maggie, and the guys took the back seats. Several other couples made the total ten.

Two of the young locals climbed up and pulled the ladder to the side then fastened it with a bungee cord to the side rails. One of the guys headed straight toward the girls: he reached over Maggie's head and knocked on the hood of the truck. He turned to take an empty seat.

"Everyone, please fasten your seat belts," he said in perfect English.

A couple of people fell for the joke and looked around for a seat belt. Maggie rolled her eyes and smiled.

"You like that one?" the man said. "I got many more to share before we end this beautiful day." He winked at the girls. "Welcome to the best jeep tour in all of Cozumel. My name is José, and this is Hose-B. We'll be your guides this beautiful day."

"It looks like it's going to rain." Kimberly had leaned over so both Maggie and Joanie could hear, but José must have overheard her. "If it rains, we get wet, but we have even more fun," he said.

They looked at each other wide eyes. "Let's pray it doesn't rain," Joanie said.

"I'm praying," Maggie said. Then she remembered her phone. "Hey, thanks for taking care of my phone," she said to

Kimberly.

"Yeah, no problem. It was David's idea, and Ralph got the rice from the kitchens. I just put it in. Did it work?"

"I didn't have time to try it. I put it on the charger before we left but haven't turned it on."

"Where did you guys go in such a hurry this morning?" Joanie asked.

"Nowhere in particular," Maggie said. "I got coffee at the café, and Mike got a few Danishes."

"He does have a sweet tooth," Joanie said, catching herself for being too familiar. "I mean, it sounds like he has a sweet tooth."

"It's worse than that," Maggie said. "Guess what he washed it down with?"

Joanie knew the answer but kept silent.

"Mountain Dew," Maggie said. "Can you believe that?"

"I believe it. Mike's from North Carolina, isn't he?" Kimberly asked.

Maggie and Joanie felt like Kimberly might have asked the question to catch them in a lie, so they stayed silent.

"Who was that hot Latin looking guy you were talking to last night?" Joanie said to change the subject.

Maggie felt her face turn hot. "I don't know who you're talking about."

"I walked by the wine bar, he was sitting with you. You looked like you knew each other."

"Oh yeah, that guy. I know him from Boca. He saw me and just stopped to say hi. I don't know him that well."

"You're from Boca?" Kimberly asked. "I thought you worked for Corporate in Charlotte."

The truck stopped in a dirt parking lot just in time. "Oh yeah, I used to live in South Florida but moved to Charlotte a few years ago."

Maggie stood, turning her body from Kimberly. She was terrible at this undercover roll; she needed to do a little more research regarding her secret identity. Using her real name probably was not a great idea either, though it wasn't like they were investigating a murder.

José and Hose-B soon had the ladder in place, and they were all standing around the well-used jeeps.

"I need two people per jeep," José said. "The color of your vehicle is your handle on the radio. I will lead, and you will follow. Please do not leave the group for any reason. Please avoid large mud holes if you can. Edwardo will bring up the rear."

"I thought his name was Hose-B?" Joanie said with a wide smile.

Mike jumped into a jeep with Joanie, and Kimberly and David naturally teamed up. Maggie felt strange to be the last one standing and looked at John sitting in the purple jeep. He motioned to her: "Your chariot awaits, my dear. Climb aboard." Maggie climbed in the seat. She looked around at the jeep. It was a metal frame welded together at a few key points. Smaller pieces of metal had been attached along the sides. Otherwise, it was completely open.

Maggie located the safety harness, pulled it across her body, and made sure it was fastened tightly.

"This ought to be fun." John was excited. He was obviously the adventurous type. Maggie looked at the welded roll bar to her right. If they flipped, would it hold, or would she die in Cozumel, Mexico, with a broken neck?

The radio broke her gloomy thoughts. *Okay, this is a radio check,"* José's voice crackled on the speaker. *"Blue, are you ready?"*

"Blue is ready," crackled David's voice.

"Big Red, you ready?"

"Big Red is ready," one of the other couples man's voice crackled.

"Pretty in Pink, check in."

The group waited while Pretty in Pink—a young girl—struggled with her radio. Finally, Hose-B left his jeep and went to help her. Still no response. Hose-B ran back to his vehicle and opened a metal toolbox. When he found what he was looking for he ran back to the young girl's jeep and fiddled with her radio. Within a minute, Pretty in Pink was acknowledging she was ready to go.

"Finally, Barney, are you ready?"

John spoke into his handset: "Barney is ready to go."

"Follow me."

José started down a gravel road at a slow speed as the other jeeps fell into line.

"I hope we're going to go faster than this," John said to Maggie as they joined the convoy, fourth in line. Joanie and Mike were just ahead, and the Pretty in Pink kids were directly behind. The young man in the passenger seat sat with his arms crossed, looking as if he was humiliated to be the only guy not at the wheel. Maggie guessed they were brother and sister and probably belonged to the couple in Big Red.

The road gradually grew narrower...the ends of the bushes reached out and tickled Maggie's arms. Before long, the trail opened up again, and the next thing Maggie knew, they were on a paved road heading through town. The group had spread farther apart as they had progressed. John would drive slowly because Pretty in Pink was lagging; then he would put on the gas full throttle until he caught up.

Maggie noted the number of identical small stucco box houses dotted across the countryside. The windows on some of the houses had bars but no glass; other windows were completely open to the elements.

"Those clothes are about to get a good rinsing," John said, pointing to full clotheslines.

"What do you mean?" Maggie asked, just as the rain started to fall.

John smiled. "Things just got interesting."

The rain was more than a shower; it was a deluge. It was like taking a shower with excellent water pressure. Maggie couldn't even talk in fear of drowning. The streets were rivers, and John was howling with joy. He slowed the jeep until he saw a large puddle and pushed the gas: they burst through the water full force, causing the water to wash over them like a wave in the middle of the ocean, momentarily blinding them to where they were relative to the other traffic.

"Remember, guys, drive carefully." José's voice crackled, but it was nearly impossible to hear him over the rain. Finally, when the deluge subsided, Maggie felt the tension drain from her body. She was thankful the water and the air were warm, because she was soaked.

After driving a short distance farther, they came to another dirt road. They turned down it and slowly made their way to a broad scenic bluff. Two picnic tables had been set up with food and drink.

Maggie unbuckled her harness and climbed down from the jeep. The view out over the sea was incredible. A hidden paradise.

"Well, that was fun," Maggie said sarcastically.

John just laughed.

Maggie took a minute to gain her composure by standing near the edge of the bluff. She took in the now clear blue sky, the turquoise water, and the mountains in the distance. The drop off in front of her was at least a hundred feet. Realizing how close she was, she took a step back, almost stepping on Mike's foot. When she turned. she saw he had two Coronas in his hand. He held one of the bottles out to her.

"This is amazing," she said. She pointed her beer toward the horizon before taking a long swallow from the bottle.

"Check that out." Mike pointed to a spot halfway down the cliff where three young men were standing. One of them bent his knees then sprang out from the cliff, diving into the clear water below. The next boy followed his friend, repeating the movements for the perfect dive.

"Wow, brave boys," Maggie said.

"I would love to join them," John said. He was standing on the other side of Maggie. He also held two beers. He seemed ready to hand Maggie one, but he noticed she already had one. When Maggie saw him pulling back she held out her empty hand.

"I'll take it," she said eagerly. John handed it to her, smiling.

She finished off the first bottle in two long drafts.

After lunch, the group loaded back into their jeeps. Maggie swapped with Joanie so she wouldn't have to think about who was going to perform her eulogy. José went through the routine of the radio checks again, and again there was a delay with Pretty in Pink even though this time, the brother had the driver's seat.

"Did you get anything out of John?" Mike asked.

"Nothing, except he obviously has a death wish. The guy loves going fast. We went through one of those puddles full throttle, completely blinded by the water, and all he did was laugh. I honestly said a prayer."

"Well, that is serious then." Mike winked at her.

"But, on the truck ride, Kimberly might have had some suspicions. Joanie and I both screwed up, acknowledging several facts about you that only someone close to you would know. It was like she was fishing, and both of us took the bait—and the hook. She might be on to us, and if she is, I'm afraid she might take additional measures to avoid exposing herself."

"Honestly, I don't think she's the one, or that she's even somehow involved," Mike said before checking in with José. He started the engine then took the second position, directly behind José.

"She was the one who hired the teller. She didn't do a background check and didn't question why the girl never came back. A total setup. I think she's the perfect suspect," Maggie said.

"A little too obvious, don't you think?" Mike asked. "She seems so much smarter than that."

"But she had access to the accounts, she could override the flags, she had the ability to pull it off."

"If she did have anything to do with it," Mike said, "I'd wager that David is one of the partners—and the mastermind;

but I think it's a good idea to keep an open mind. In my experience, most of the time the most obvious suspect is the actual perpetrator."

"You think David is the most obvious suspect?"

"That's not exactly what I'm saying. I just think he's the smartest one out of all of them. I'm actually beginning to think that the real culprit is a professional not even associated with the bank."

"But they had to have some help, right?" Maggie asked. She watched Mike nod his head before she sat back in her seat. The sun was shining as if the rain had never washed through the countryside. She enjoyed the view much better on the ride back as Mike took it slow and avoided potholes along the way.

Once they reached the truck José thanked the group for joining them on their adventure as Hose-B unfasted the ladder. He took his position at the bottom, holding a bucket with *TIPS* written in black marker.

CHAPTER 11

Captain's Table

Dinnertime arrived. Maggie wore a long blue off-the-shoulder number that didn't entirely hide the extra pounds in the middle, but the long slit on the side showed off her long legs and the neckline exposed just enough cleavage to be distracting. Mike had dressed in the guys' room to give her space, so when she made her entrance all three men turned at once. They stared with open mouths like she was the first woman they had ever seen.

Maggie's face turned hot. "What?" she asked.

"You look…incredible," Mike said.

John shook his head. "Wow. Maggie. A head-turner."

"You don't look like the same person," David added.

Maggie rolled her eyes. "Thanks, that's a compliment, I guess."

Just then the girls' door opened, and Joanie and Kimberly walked into the living area. They both looked beautiful. Joanie was wearing a short red dress with matching red heels. Her dark hair piled on top of her head, with just a few curls hanging loose. She looked elegant. But Kimberly stole the show. She wore a light teal gown that accentuated every curve of her body. She looked like a contestant for a pageant. Her high cheekbones and full lips combined with the red hair she had pulled away from her face. She was stunning. Maggie was glad she had come out first, so she had attracted at least a little attention.

Maggie watched Kimberly move across the floor. If she

would just smile, she would be the most beautiful woman Maggie had ever seen, but her forced smile and her slumped shoulders showed some kind of insecurity. Could it be guilt weighing her down? Maggie knew this girl was going to be hard to crack.

"You look amazing." Mike took Maggie's arm.

"You already said that."

Maggie felt like she was at a homecoming dance, minus the corsage. Being so close to Mike, she could smell his cologne. A fresh spicy scent…not Old Spice. Maggie remembered the first time she had met him, and how disappointed she was that he was wearing a wedding ring…and how relieved she was to learn he wore it only as a distraction for his investigations. He told her it helped him do his job: people trusted a married man more than a single guy.

"You look pretty dapper yourself," Maggie told Mike, to take the edge off her earlier response. As she walked, she found herself measuring her steps. It had been a while since she had worn heels; she didn't want to turn an ankle.

Ralph appeared with a tray of champagne glasses, offering them to the group. "You all look fabulous," he said. Each took their glass.

"Thank you, Ralph," Mike said as Ralph backed off, leaving the group gathered in a circle.

"Well, cheers," John said.

"Cheers," everyone repeated.

John downed the entire glass in one go. By the time he finished, Ralph reappeared with an open bottle, ready to refill his glass.

Maggie took a sip from her glass then set it on the counter behind her.

"I sure miss happy hour with the girls," she said to Mike. No one was near enough to hear her.

"I'm not trying to be judgmental, but it seemed like you girls lives revolved around alcoholic beverages."

"Sounds a little judgmental to me, but I tell you this, I can't wait to get back behind those gates and leave reality behind. It's like an escape from a world of turbulence, stress, and responsibilities. I just need a game of golf and a happy hour with my friends."

"Does that satisfy you?" Mike asked.

"Definitely."

"What about real companionship?"

"I have my girls and my other friends at the club."

"I'm talking about real, meaningful relationships."

"Oh, you're talking about those relationships that provide hurt, disappointment, and betrayal. I think I've had enough of those in my life. I'm good."

"Hmm, you sound more cynical than good."

"It's called self-preservation, Mike. One thing about me is I am a survivor."

"I see." Mike felt concerned, but he let it settle to consider later.

"Let's go have some fun."

Maggie put her arm through Mike's. David took Kimberly's arm. John escorted Joanie through the door and down the hall to the elevator.

*

Entering the formal dining room was an event in itself. The dining room encompassed several levels of seating. A crystal chandelier hung over the vast open space of the central area, spreading flickers of light like small fairies floating through the room. Classical music played softly in the background; the music combined with crystalline sounds of tinkling glassware, contributed to the magical feeling. Smiling passengers dressed in their finest were escorted graciously to their tables. Just as Maggie's small group stepped in the doorway, they were greeted by Captain Dillard. He sported his most formal uniform, complete with gold braiding and tight creases.

The captain escorted Maggie and the others to a platform suspended between the two lower levels. It was like a private dining area set among hundreds of other tables.

Kimberly was the first to take her seat. Maggie quickly sat

next to her.

Kimberly turned to the steward. "I think we should sit boy-girl, don't you?" It was more of a statement than a question.

"Wherever you like, madam," the steward replied.

Maggie took the hint. She slid over to the next chair, leaving an open chair between herself and Kimberly. Kimberly signaled for David to sit next to her.

"Welcome to the captain's table," Captain Dillard announced as the last two guests arrived. "Unfortunately, I will not be able to join you tonight, but you will find yourselves in good hands. May I introduce our head of security, Randolph Edwards, and our beautiful cruise director, Jules Gilbert."

Randolph and Mike took seats on opposite sides of Maggie. Joanie sat next to Mike. John held a chair for Jules to take her seat, and then he sat right next to her.

The steward moved around the table, placing the napkins in the laps of each of the guests as the captain proceeded to address the table.

"Tonight we have a special treat. I have invited Alfonzo Martin, one of only two hundred and two master sommeliers in the world, to your table this evening. As Chef Paul provides his culinary masterpieces, Alfonzo will pair each course with the perfect wine. I wish you all a fabulous evening and an unforgettable dining experience."

The Captain moved aside as both Chef Paul and a handsome Latin man appeared from a side door, as if on cue. The table followed the captain's lead in lightly applauding their arrival. Chef Paul wore the same white executive chef's clothing had had worn the day before. Alfonzo sported black pants, a white dress shirt with an open collar, and a buttoned-up black vest. He stood with a posture that would make any mother proud.

"Again, welcome to my table. I know you will have a wonderful meal, bon appetite." Captain Dillard bowed slightly then moved on to other tables as he made his way through the dining room.

"Welcome to the captain's table this evening," Alfonzo began. "Tonight we try something a little different. We learn about wine and food and, most importantly, how the two come together for a wonderful experience." He smiled at the group. "Are you ready for a great experience?"

The group sat silently, nodding their heads.

"Such a lively group," Alfonzo said sarcastically. He pointed to the table. "You will each see five glasses sitting in front of you. With each course prepared by your very own Chef Paul, a sample of the perfect wine I have personally selected will be served.."

"Awesome," Maggie said.

Picking up on the audience participation, Alfonzo pointed at Maggie. "Yes, awesome. So let's get started, shall we?" He signaled to the server, who was standing by.

While they were waiting for the first uncorking, Mike took the opportunity to start a conversation with John.

"So, John, at the muster station drill, you were telling us you were a marine...?"

John sat straight as if he was ready for duty. "Yes, sir, MAR-SOC."

"A Raider?" Mike also sat up straight. "Impressive."

"'MARSOC'?" Maggie asked.

"Special Ops," Mike answered. "I was also in the corps, military police."

"I spent over ten years until this." John pointed to his leg. "I was forced out with early retirement."

"I'm sorry, man," Mike said. "Honestly, you can hardly tell you have a limp."

"One thing I learned in Desert Storm, never take life for granted, you know," John said.

"I hear you, man, that life takes a toll."

"Well, Desert Storm was mild compared to what I found when I came back home. My wife had found another guy, sold my house, and emptied my bank accounts. I came home to nothing," John said.

"Jeez, man, why did she do that?"

"I guess she thought I was dead," he said, smiling. Then he leaned over to whisper a few words into Jules' ear that made her laugh.

The first course was presented by three servers, each holding two small plates that they set, in unison, before the seated guests. Maggie looked down at her plate. A small orange ball of cantaloupe was wrapped in prosciutto and drizzled with balsamic vinegar. The servers then poured each diner a fourth of a glass of light white wine.

"A beautiful California sauvignon blanc," Alfonzo explained, picking up a glass of wine he had poured himself. "I'm not sure who among you has extensive experience with wine; if you are a novice I hope the next few hours will allow you to discover a new passion for wine. The selection before you costs anywhere from twenty to twenty-five dollars a bottle. Does anyone know the difference between a twenty-five-dollar bottle of wine and a fifty-dollar bottle of wine?"

Maggie raised her hand. Alfonzo pointed at her. "Young lady."

"The year?"

"It could be the year...anyone else?"

No one took the bait.

"Often the difference between a twenty-five-dollar bottle of wine and a fifty-dollar bottle of wine is...twenty-five dollars. It's not always the price that differentiates a great bottle of wine."

Mike shook his head and smiled at Maggie. She almost always ordered the house Cabernet, saying there just wasn't enough difference.

"The first thing we must do is address the wine," Alfonzo continued. He held his glass by the stem. "Use your eyes to examine the color and texture of the liquid. Now, slowly bring it to your nose, tipping it approximately thirty degrees, placing the lip of the glass just above your top lip."

David picked up his glass "Well, how do you do?" he said.

Some giggles floated around the table, but quickly the group followed Alfonzo's lead. "Now move the glass away so that it is no longer touching your lip. Now, breathe in through both your nose and your mouth... The light, fruity, flowery aroma lives at the very top, so take care not to dip your nose below the rim of the glass. If your nose dips too deep, you will miss the fragrance."

"It's a little citrusy," Kimberly said.

"Aw, good nose, my dear. The citrus undertones will bring out the fresh flavor of the melon combined with the salty pro-sciutto and the balsamic, which has also been aged in an oak barrel. It is perfect."

The group again followed Alfonzo's actions, cutting the appetizer in half, taking a bite and then a sip of the wine.

"Wow," Joanie said, that's amazing."

The servers quickly took the empty plates and glasses then replaced them with new ones. Again Maggie examined her plate: poached Maine lobster served with a cakebread Chardon-nay.

"I can taste the butter," Maggie said.

"Exactly," Alfonzo said. "Cakebread also is a California wine and is about fifty dollars a bottle. It pairs splendidly with the lobster."

The group fell quiet, enjoying the taste of the lobster and the buttery Chardonnay. When the next plate had been set in front of each diner, Maggie looked at it suspiciously.

"A sweet foie gras sitting on lovely spinach and topped with mustard seeds. A special treat! With this dish, we have a beautiful Chateau Bonnet Rose from the Bordeaux region of France."

Maggie pushed her plate away. "Don't eat that," she whis-pered to Mike.

"Why?" he whispered back.

"It's goose liver. They force feed the poor animal for weeks just to get the liver to taste like that. It's definably animal cruelty."

"Are you serious?"

"One hundred percent. *Don't* eat it." This time she had whispered too loud. Randolph leaned into her.

"Why?" he whispered back.

"It's goose liver. They torture the poor creature by force feeding it with a tube to fatten it up."

"Seriously?" But Randolph had spoken too loudly. Everyone at the table looked over curiously. He pushed his plate away from him in disgust. "I don't like liver of any kind."

"I admit this is not a delicacy for an unsophisticated palette," Alfonzo said.

Maggie whispered to Randolph: "I think he just called us unsophisticated."

"You can call me anything you want, but hell if I'll touch that mess," Randolph said just as the server picked up his plate.

Somehow the way Randolph had expressed his disgust struck Maggie as funny. She smiled, feeling some of the effects of the wine. Mike took a sip of each wine the servers had poured then handed Maggie the rest of his glass.

The final course was filet mignon settled into a bed of golden mashed potatoes topped with a béarnaise sauce. One of the servers set the dish in front of both Maggie and Randolph simultaneously. Randolph leaned over and said, "Looks like someone shit on those mashed potatoes."

Maggie couldn't contain herself. She covered her mouth until she couldn't hold it in any longer. She let out a laugh, causing Randolph also to laugh. But Maggie couldn't contain herself.

"What is so funny?" Mike asked.

"He said…he said…"

Maggie couldn't get any more words out. She held her stomach and covered her mouth, trying to squelch her laughter. Everyone else at the table stared at the two.

"What is so funny?" Kimberly asked.

"I can't…"

Tears were coming from Randolph's eyes; he, too, was holding his stomach. Maggie tried to get a hold of herself, but every time she looked at her plate, she started laughing again. The rest of the table began laughing in sympathy but sincerely wanted to know what was so funny. Finally, Maggie left the table. She found the nearest restroom and splashed cold water on her face. Kimberly and Joanie walked in, just as Maggie finally gained her composure.

"What was so funny?" Joanie asked.

"It wasn't just what he said; it was how he said it," Maggie said.

Kimberly looked impatient with her hands on her hips. "What did he say?"

"He said"—Maggie wiped her face with a paper towel—"'looks like someone shit on those mash potatoes.'"

"Gross," Joanie said.

"It kind of did look like that," Kimberly said, smiling.

"I guess it's even funnier because of who said it. Randolph seems like such a serious guy, and he just leaned over and said it so deadpan." Maggie giggled a bit but quickly regained her composure. "Okay, I'm good. Let's go eat our shit," she said, shaking her head.

When the three women returned to the table, the other members of the group were busy eating their filets. Maggie was super excited that her wine glass was full.

"It's a Camus Cabernet," Mike said, "so I had them go ahead and fill it."

"That's why I love you." Maggie smiled—but then she panicked. "You know what I mean. I don't *love* love you…you know, as a friend loves a—"

"Maggie." Mike stopped her. "It's good. Drink your wine."

Maggie picked up her glass and didn't bother addressing the wine or breathing in the aroma. She just went for the magic of the soothing oaky taste of her favorite wine. She couldn't look at Randolph, fearing the giggles would come back, but she pushed away from her steak.

Alfonzo appeared again. "And the finale…" He raised his arms as though he was about to perform a magic trick. The finale was a baseball-sized chocolate-covered ice cream dessert accompanied by a small gravy boat of hot chocolate syrup.

"Now, pour the syrup over the dish," Chef Paul instructed.

As each member of the group poured, the frozen chocolate mound on their plate melted away, exposing the vanilla ice cream sitting on a thick chocolate brownie. It was chocolate heaven.

"The only thing that makes this dessert more perfect is the Portugal late bottled vintage port." Alfonzo stood with a huge smile. His performance had come to an end. "I thank each of you for an unforgettable evening."

"Thank you," each of the diners said as Alfonzo backed away. He disappeared through the side door.

"That was incredible," David said.

"It was pretty cool," Mike agreed, "even though I'm not much of a wine drinker."

Jules chimed in. "Your group was one of the best groups we've had the pleasure of having the captain's dinner with."

"So, it's the captain's table dinner—but no captain?" David asked.

"True," Jules said. "But this captain never eats with the passengers, he eats with his crew. He assigns some of the executive staff to represent him." The next moment she changed the topic. "You all should join our Newlyweds Game on Sea Day."

"We aren't couples," Joanie said.

"Oh, my bad." Jules smiled. "But that might be even more fun."

"I had a great time." Randolph stood, placing a gentle hand on Maggie's shoulder. "Sorry if I offended anyone."

"It's all good," Mike said. He stood to reach behind Maggie to shake Randolph's hand. "It was fun."

"Anyone up for the casino?" John asked.

"I'm in," Joanie said.

"Me too," Mike said.

"I'm going to bed," Maggie said. "It's an early start tomorrow in Belize."

"I'm going to take a walk around the ship," Kimberly informed the others. "I think I've gained ten pounds since we got on this ship."

"I'll join you, if you don't mind," David said.

They left the table, heading in different directions. As soon as Maggie reached the suite and changed into her pajamas, she pulled out her phone and called Britney.

TUESDAY

CHAPTER 12

Maggie was one of the first passengers off the ship. She boarded the water taxi that tendered her and only two other couples to Tourism Village in Belize City. She had finally checked her phone. She had several messages from Alex and Britney.

Alex's messages assured her that Silas and Jay weren't working for her, and Britney was bringing her the notebook. She wasn't sure what was in the notebook or why the guys were asking about it. She told Maggie to be safe.

Britney's message was the biggest surprise. As soon as Maggie reached the end of the pier, she spotted Britney. She was wearing her Louis Vuitton sunglasses and had flung her matching oversized bag over her shoulder. She waved to Maggie. Maggie wanted to run into her friend's arms, but she remained calm. She increased her stride purposefully until she reached her friend's open arms. Maggie hugged Britney as if she hadn't seen her in years instead of weeks.

"Girl, you need a drink?"

"It's a little early," Maggie said, smiling. "I feel like I'm in a foreign country."

"You are in a foreign country," Britney said.

"Well, yeah." She smiled. "I missed you. I miss Alex. I miss my house and my pool and my life in Boca."

"Boca misses you too, but right now just follow me." Britney led her into the street. where a smartly dressed black man stood next to a black sedan. "This is Terrance."

"Hi, Terrance," Maggie said, smiling and shaking his hand. "Nice to meet you."

"And you, Maggie. Britney has told me so much about you."

"She has?" Maggie smiled, turning to Britney. "How long have you been here?"

"Two days. Terrance owns the hotel I'm looking at for my next big job."

"Aw, nice," Maggie said.

Britney designed high-end hotel lobbies for boutique hotels all over the world. She was the youngest member at Banyan Tree Country Club, and the prettiest. For those two reasons, she had a hard time "fitting in" at the club. The first time she and Maggie had met, they were instant friends even though Britney could have been Maggie's daughter.

"I haven't purchased the property quite yet," Terrence said as he opened the sedan's back door for the ladies. But Britney has given me hope that the place can be transformed into something extraordinary."

"You're the one with the great ideas," Britney said. "I just sprinkle a little magic on it." She slid into the back seat, motioning Maggie to scoot in next to her.

"So tourism is good?" Maggie asked as she slid in.

"Better every day," Terrance said, "but this hotel will cater to a very exclusive clientele." He shut the back door then climbed into the driver's seat.

"This place is beautiful," Maggie said as they drove through several side streets along the ocean's edge.

"It's amazing," Britney said, also looking out the window.

Before long Terrance pulled the car through a gate leading to what looked like a mansion rather than a hotel.

"It's unbelievable," Maggie said.

She followed Terrance and Britney as they led her through a side gate to the ocean side of the hotel. The view was breathtaking. She could see her cruise ship in the distance.

"It's very exclusive," Britney said.

Terrance led them to a small tiki hut where they set their feet in the white sand.

"What time do we need to get you back?" Terrance asked.

Maggie smiled. "I have to be back by two o'clock to catch the water taxi."

"Okay, you ladies have a good visit. I'll be in the office if you need anything."

"I'm so glad you met me here," Maggie said to Britney after Terrance had left. "What a great surprise."

"I was supposed to come next month. Terrance has been negotiating with the owner and happened to be here when I called. Terrance is ready to sign but is holding out not to act too eager because he wants the place next door too. He was thrilled I could come early, and we've come up with some amazing concepts. Now all he has to do is get the boss's approval, and we can schedule the transformation."

"He has a boss? I thought he was the owner."

"His wife," Britney said, smiling. "But now spill…How is your boyfriend?"

"Number one, Mike is *not* my boyfriend, even though I told him I loved him last night."

"What?"

"Well, not that I loved-love him…Ugh. Never mind."

"You are a crazy girl, Maggie McFarlin," Britney said.

Just then a waiter set two large mango margaritas on the small table in front of them.

"Oh Lord, it's only ten a.m."

"It's actually only nine seventeen, but you are technically on vacation, so drink up," Britney said. She held the big glass for Maggie to acknowledge. "Cheers.""Cheers, baby girl."

They clinked glasses before taking a drink from the paper straws.

Maggie watched Britney dig through her purse until she came up with a Tiffany-blue pouch. She quickly unfolded the pouch and retrieved a glass straw from the pocket. Then she took the paper straw out of her drink and replaced it with the glass Tiffany straw. "Much better," she said. Britney stirred her drink with the glass straw. "I saw Alex yesterday in New York."

"She left me a voice mail and said that you gave her the notebook. But how is she doing?"

"They cleared her of having anything to do with Marco's murder, thanks to the recorded admission recovered from your phone. She's going to have someone go through the notebook to see if there's something we missed."

"I'm just glad that is all over," Maggie said.

"Yeah, but remember when Angie was run over by her loser husband, and Alex picked up her purse?"

"Yes?"

"Well, Alex found this."

Britney handed Maggie a manilla envelope.

"It was in Angie's purse. It seems like Marco was going to use it to get more money from you."

Maggie began unfastening the butterfly closure. "What is it?" Britney put her hand on top of Maggie's to stop her from opening it.

"Don't open it right now. I looked, and I think you should wait. It's not bad. Well, honestly, I don't know if it's bad or not. Maybe it's kind of emotionally bad. I don't want to say more. I just think if you could just wait, it would be better."

"Okay..."

Maggie looked worried but folded the large manilla envelope and zipped it into the backpack she had slung over the chair. Her curiosity was raw. She needed to refocus on why she was meeting Britney here.

"Are you ready to find out all about your boyfriend's sister?" Britney said, sensing Maggie's distracted mind.

One of the texts Maggie had sent to Britney asked if she could find out any background information on Joanie. There was something that Joanie wasn't telling them, and Maggie couldn't discuss this subject with Mike, who seemed overly protective of his sister.

"I have to know what's in that envelope," Maggie said, reaching back in the backpack.

"Okay, I guess you should open it up, but then you won't hear any information I spent good money getting for you." Britney placed her hand on the envelope, which was now sitting on the table.

"You're right." Maggie shifted her gaze from the table to Britney. "Tell me what you found out."

"Joanie Brown was born Janet Joanne Marker. She was born in nineteen seventy-three to Darlene and William Marker. She was probably an unexpected gift since they were both well into their forties when she was born; her brother, Mike Marker, was nine years old. She was an average student until junior high when she was caught shoplifting multiple times. It appears her parents had no control over her. She was also involved in drugs and ran away until her parents finally gave up. She was pregnant at sixteen. That's when Mike came home and left the marines. He stayed, and his parents moved to Boca Raton."

Maggie did the math in her head. "That kid would be thirty years old. That's weird. Mike has never mentioned a thirty-year-old niece or nephew."

"That's probably because he was given up for adoption," Britney said.

"She gave her baby up for adoption?"

"No, she gave *both* her babies up for adoption. As soon as she had that one, she was pregnant again. She gave the second one to the same adoptive parents as the first one."

"I wonder if she knows the kids?"

"I don't know. What I do know is at seventeen, Joanie ended up in juvie for armed robbery."

"What? That's a felony. How does she work at the bank?"

"I don't know how he did it, but Mike got her record expunged or sealed or something because the crime doesn't show anywhere."

"How did you find out about it?"

"One of her school friends knew about it, and my private

detective talked to one of the guards that used to work at the juvenile facility. Anyway, it was the boyfriend who was the actual perp; Janet claimed he forced her to drive the car. But when there's a gun involved, all the participants are charged with *armed* robbery instead of robbery. The guy was in prison but got out last month."

"I wonder if she knows about that?"

"I would say yes. Joanie visited him on and off throughout the years. Most likely he's the father of the first two children that were adopted."

"What about the two children she has now? I think one is fifteen and—"

"Not sure how it happened, but when the guy went to prison, she seemed to straighten up, she got her G-E-D and went to college, where she earned a degree in business. She started working at the bank as soon as she turned eighteen. She worked through college, starting as a janitor then working up to a teller and now head honcho. As successful as she was at work, she still had challenges in her relationships. Her ex-husband was another real loser."

"Yeah, Mike filled me in on that situation."

"She was a shit show who turned around to be a productive member of society, squeaky clean."

"Well, thanks for the info. I guess I feel better that I got drug into this," Maggie said. "Anything on the aunt?"

"Nothing."

Maggie picked up the envelope. "Can I look at this now?"

Britney shook her head in disapproval. "If you insist."

Maggie carefully unfolded the top edge. Inside was a single piece of paper. She brought it out and examined it.

"A birth certificate?" she said.

"Yep," Britney confirmed. She had already looked at it.

"I don't get it," Maggie said/ "Should this mean something to me?"

"Look at the birth date?"

"March twenty-seventh, nineteen sixty-three. The same

day I was born."

"Yes."

"Britney, help me out here," Maggie said, "should I know this person?"

"Oh my god, Maggie, it's you. That is your birth certificate." She pointed to the name on the official form.

"This is *not* my birth certificate. I've seen my birth certificate, and this isn't it. Why do you think it is?"

"This was in Angie's handbag that night she was meeting with us. That and the life insurance policy with her name on it. According to Alex, Marco was going to use it to get some money from your parents. He must have thought you were from money."

"I guess he must have figured it out—but honestly, this isn't me. I'm one hundred percent sure. If you saw my father, you wouldn't have a doubt. I look just like him."

"There is no father listed on this birth certificate," Britney pointed out.

"Why do you think this is me?" Maggie asked again. "It doesn't make sense. If it was me—and it isn't—how did Marco come up with this?"

"I don't know. Alex gave it to me when I was with her in New York. She said to give it to you when you got back to Boca. I guess I should have waited."

"No, no. It's okay, really." Maggie saw the anguish on Britney's face. "I appreciate that you gave this to me, and I'm not upset. I just think it's a mistake, but I'll look into it."

"Okay, I didn't want you to freak out," Britney said.

"I'm a little freaked out, but I'm glad you gave it to me."

"What are your new friends doing today?" Britney asked to refocus Maggie's brain.

"Mike and Joanie are going cave tubing, and Kimberly and David are zip-lining. I think John is rock climbing."

"Sounds fun," Britney said. "Too bad you had to waste your day with me."

"I'd much rather be here with you, and honestly, I can't

wait to get back to my life in Boca. We need a night out at Capital Grill. I've been craving some French onion soup." Maggie smiled at her friend as she tucked the birth certificate back into the envelope then zipped it into her backpack.

"That does sound yummy. Speaking of yummy, what's the scoop on Mikey?" Britney said. She set her elbows on the table and folded her hands under her chin gazing at Maggie at full attention.

"Hate to disappoint, but there is nothing to tell." Maggie's voice dropped. "Unfortunately."

"Maybe Miss Maggie needs to make the first move," Britney suggested.

"I like him, but it's not going to work out. He has a whole life in Mayberry."

"Hahaha. That's funny. But seriously, why not have some fun and go home?"

"He's not that kind of guy,"

"Sister, *every* guy is that kind of guy, unless..."

"Unless what?"

"Unless he likes you...like you're *the one* and all that."

"HA!" Maggie said too loudly. Then, in a more calm voice: "If he even thought of me as more than a friend, other than in the most platonic way possible, he sure hides it well. So if we are going down a road, he's sticking to the 'friend's zone.'"

"I hate to tell you, Maggie, but when it comes to harmless flirting, you are so obvious like a chatty Kathy, but when you're seriously interested, you freeze up like a mannequin."

Maggie frowned. "It's awkward, especially since we're staying in the same room. I can't even—"

"Wait, *wait*." Britney smiled wide. "You are sharing a room?"

"We have to, the couple we replaced were married. There wasn't an option."

"You are telling me that there wasn't one empty cabin on that giant monster of a ship?"

"Well yeah, but..."

"Maggie, Maggie, Maggie."

"What?"

"The opportunity is there, now take it."

"I can't even sleep. I'm so afraid I'm going to snore."

"That's unfortunately true. I've shared a room with you, and snoring is only half of it. Woman, you yell and scream and fight in your sleep."

Maggie's face heated up. She thought her night terrors were under control.

"I'm sorry," Maggie said, hanging her head.

"You don't have to be sorry. I never said anything because I didn't want to embarrass you." Britney put a hand on Maggie's shoulder.

"But you tell me now?"

"You're sleeping in the same room as the man you might want to marry."

"Oh my! Britney." Maggie felt her face go slack. She wanted to cry, both from embarrassment and the flood of memories rushing into her head.

"Another drink?" Britney asked at the same time she waved for the server.

"Or ten," Maggie said.

Alcohol was the only way to forget the past. She had once gone to a therapist who asked her if she had ever been in combat. When Maggie asked why, the therapist told her she had severe PTSD. Maggie couldn't come up with any horrific event in her life, so the therapist wanted to try to hypnotize her. That was her last appointment. Instead, Maggie quit her job, moved from the rain in Seattle to the sunshine in Boca. It was the best therapy. She could breathe again. Life was good.

After several more drinks disappeared in front of them, Terrance reappeared. He delivered Maggie back to the pier, where she and Britney hugged.

"Have fun on the rest of the trip. I'll see you back home next week."

It was always as if Britney was the older woman in the relationship.

"'K, love you, Brit."

"Love you, Maggs. Now go have fun."

Maggie swung the backpack over her shoulder and turned to wave at Terrance and Britney as they stood watching her make her way down the pier. She measured her steps, feeling the effects of the alcohol.

The water taxi was full, but Maggie was able to squeeze in as the last one aboard. She considered waiting for the next taxi, but instead stood with her back to the other passengers and held on to the pole, facing the ocean.

She let the sea air hit her face, closed her eyes, feeling the motion of the waves as they traveled the short distance. Because she was the last on, she was the first off, letting her walk fast and allowing her to be the first on the gangway, out of the crowd.

She placed her backpack on the conveyer belt and went through the metal detector. The elevator was empty; she rode straight up to Deck 11 and stepped into her suite. Ralph welcomed her back, and she took her favorite seat by the window. He handed her a glass of Cabernet, which she took a sip of before setting it on the side table.

She unzipped the backpack and took the birth certificate from the envelope. Free from Britney's supervision, she took the time to read every line. The mother's name: Sarah Anne Marshall. The birth date: March 27, 1963, her birthday. But the baby's name was Anne Louise Marshall....Did it mean anything that Maggie's middle name was Anne, or was that a coincidence? Where the father's name should have been was typed UNKNOWN, all in capital letters, like a neon sign advertising the insult. The birthplace was listed as St. Joseph's hospital in downtown Tacoma, Washington. It was an official copy complete with an embossed state seal. Maggie ran her fingers over the raised letters as if she could feel something familiar.

The door into the suite clicked...the gang had returned. Maggie returned the paper to the envelope then set it back into her backpack; then she got back to her wine. The group became busy recollecting their adventures among each other, but Maggie wasn't one bit envious. She took another drink of her wine.

CHAPTER 13

"Ladies, get ready, we have the slot tournament qualifying rounds," Kimberly announced as she rushed into the common space where everyone was lounging.

"I am *not* in the mood," Maggie complained.

"Well, you better get in the mood," Joanie said. She pulled Maggie to her feet. "We have a reservation at the Mexican place and then off to the casino."

Maggie was looking forward to dinner. She enjoyed the formal dining room, but Chi Chi's was her all-time favorite restaurant in West Palm Beach—and why not? She especially liked the tableside preparation of the guacamole and the freshly made margaritas. The restaurant was famous for never using a mix. All ingredients were fresh and organic.

When they arrived at the restaurant on Deck 4, it looked identical to the location in Palm Beach. Sugar skulls and vibrant colored tapestries hung from the walls. A table for six awaited them. The ladies sat at one end and the guys perched themselves at the other.

As soon as the waiter arrived, Maggie took the lead. She ordered the tableside guacamole, the bacon-wrapped shrimp appetizer, and fresh margaritas for everyone. She noticed the shocked look on everyone's face as ordered for them.

"Seriously, just trust me," she said. "If you don't like the margaritas you can order something else, but at least give it a try. I'm not a huge fan of tequila, but this 'rita is to die for."

David pushed a stack of pretend casino chips onto the table. "I'm all in."

Kimberly drew the restaurant's giant menu close to her face. "Whatever."

"No salt on mine," Maggie told the waiter.

The waiter looked around the table for confirmation. Mike acknowledged his approval, circling his index finger through the air. The waiter slipped his notebook into his front apron pocket then motioned for another server nearby who was pushing a cart full of ingredients for fresh guacamole.

He set the small cart near the table and started scooping avocadoes into a massive bowl. He added tomato, onion, cilantro, and a little salt and pepper. He mixed the ingredients in the massive bowl then divided the freshly made guacamole into two equal portions. He scooped each portion into a smaller bowl. He placed one of the smaller bowls at each end of the table just as a third server arrived, setting a basket of warm tortilla chips on the table.

The table turned quiet as the group enjoyed the appetizer. Then the margaritas arrived. Joanie decided to make a toast. She stood and said: "Here's to a great team. All of you guys made this trip possible by being the best of the best. Thank you for all your hard work and dedication." She raised her heavy glass. "Cheers!"

"Cheers!" everyone repeated.

Joanie sat down, but her smile turned flat and her eyes lost focus. She looked down almost as if she was going to cry. Maggie thought maybe she was losing confidence that she and Mike would figure out what happened to her aunt's money; most likely it would never be recovered. She would not only lose her job but her reputation, and she might face criminal charges. The future didn't look good for Joanie.

"Have you been in a slot tournament before?" Maggie asked, hoping to break Joanie's thoughts.

Joanie's face lit up. "I have," she said. "It's a lot of fun."

"What's the secret to winning?" Kimberly asked, engaging in the conversation.

"There's one simple strategy," Joanie said slyly. "Push the button as many times as you can."

"That's it? It doesn't sound very competitive," Kimberly said.

"You'll see, you get caught up in the whole thing. Just remember to set your machine to bet MAX every time and play all the pay lines and push that button as many times as you can."

"So, basically, everyone has the same opportunity to win?" Maggie said.

"But there is a winner." Again Joanie lit up. "A ten-thousand-dollar winner."

"I didn't hear that part when we signed up," Kimberly said, taking a long drink from her margarita. "I thought it was a free cruise or something."

"The top five all win free cruises. You must not have been paying attention when we signed up," Joanie said.

"Ten thousand?" Kimberly said. "I'm paying attention now."

Dinner arrived. The conversation focused on what each of the ladies would buy with the ten thousand dollars if they won the tournament.

"I might buy my son a car," Joanie said.

"I would probably take a trip to Italy or Paris—I just want to travel," Kimberly said. "What about you, Maggie?"

"I would probably just save it for a rainy day." She was thinking that Kimberly could do a lot of traveling with a million dollars.

They finished up dinner and headed for the casino.

"Maybe I shouldn't have had two margaritas," Joanie said. "My head is feeling a little light." She had obviously forgotten whatever was troubling her earlier.

"I feel nice and relaxed, ready to go," Kimberly said.

The three guys followed the ladies; they were chatting about some football team or baseball team. As they entered the casino, the ladies followed the signs to a roped-off section of the slot area. They picked machines next to each other. Maggie was at the end, Joanie in the middle, and then Kimberly. Three other passengers were sitting at the other end, six others had selected machines on the other side of their machines, and six sat directly behind them.

"Okay, ladies and gentlemen"—Jules walked between the machines, speaking into a microphone—"welcome to round one of the Official Cruise Slot Tournament." A small crowd started to assemble to watch the spectacle. "The round consists of two-fifteen minute sessions; the top three scores from both sessions progress to the finals, which will take place this same time tomorrow. You must remain at your machine the entire time. No use of phones or electronics is allowed while playing. If you leave your machine at any time during the round, you will forfeit your score. Does anyone have any questions?"

No one spoke; instead, everyone placed their hands on the buttons of their slot machine.

"Are you ready?" Jules said.

A yell rose up from the players: "Yes!"

"Then let's get playing—GO!"

The machines lit up. The noise was almost deafening. Maggie focused on her machine, pushing the button every time it stopped. She noticed Joanie's quick movements and tried to copy her. Joanie's slot machine seemed to *bing* and *buzz* more frequently—and more loudly—than Maggie's. It wasn't until the end of the round that Maggie stood up and realized it hadn't been Joanie who had been scoring so much, it was Kimberly.

Jules and several assistants recorded the scores for each player. "You have fifteen minutes before round two," she announced, releasing them for a break. "Don't be late."

Maggie closed her eyes, waiting for the crowd to dissipate before heading over to the bar set up in the middle of the casino. "I'll have a Cabernet," she told the bartender just as he set a cocktail napkin in front of her. He nodded his head and reached for a wine glass hanging on a rack above them.

As she took the first sip of her wine, Maggie noticed John

sitting on the opposite side of the bar, chatting with one of the bartenders. They were leaning in close to each other, as if they didn't want anyone to hear what they were saying. When the bartender stood, Maggie was shocked. The man could have been John's brother. He was the same height, and he was bald, just like John. It was only when the bartender turned around that the difference became clear. The man had a broader nose and a definite scar across the bottom of his chin. He looked like he should have been the bouncer rather than a bartender.

Maggie grabbed her wine and hurried back to her machine. Five minutes remained until the next session began. Joanie had not yet returned.

"Nice job there, Kimberly," Maggie said.

"I have to admit, that was fun." She smiled. "I think the margaritas helped. I had a rhythm going."

Joanie took her seat. "Okay, ladies, good luck on this round."

The three ladies high-fived each other.

The second session began as the first one had. The machines lit up, and the buzzing and ringing started. Maggie tried to focus on pushing her buttons but became distracted. She looked up just as the bartender who had been talking to John left the casino.

Maggie continued pushing the buttons until she noticed John also exiting the casino. She looked around for Mike but didn't see him. She pushed her buttons a few more times until curiosity took over. She stood from her seat in front of the slot machine and left to follow John. If Joanie and Kimberly noticed they didn't show any concern: they were concentrating on pushing the buttons. Maggie looked for Mike one last time as she moved through the casino. She finally spotted him across the room at the roulette wheel.

There was no time to tell Mike what she was doing; she would lose John if she didn't follow him. Keeping a safe distance, Maggie watched John enter the elevator. After the doors closed she kept her eyes on the monitor over the doors. The elevator stopped three decks above her. Instead of waiting for the elevator to return, Maggie ran up the stairs. When she reached the top, she could hardly breathe but leaned on the bulkhead near the deck schematic.

Staterooms took up most of the deck, but a business center was located on the starboard side. Maggie walked slowly, still trying to catch her breath until she reached a large door with a glass window. She glanced in the room behind the door and saw the bartender sitting in front of a computer, tapping the keyboard. John was leaning over the bartender's shoulder. After a few moments he walked to the printer and removed a few pages from the printing tray. The bartender stood, and suddenly Maggie knew it was time to go. She ducked into the steward's closet nearby until the two came out of the computer room and passed by. Then she stuck her head out to see if the coast was clear. The bartender turned just in time to see her but then turned back and continued to walk away.

Maggie waited a few more minutes before she felt secure enough to leave the closet. She walked to the bank of elevators and rode back down the three decks. She found the nearest restroom and splashed water on her face to cool down before returning to the casino. The bartender was back behind the bar. He looked up as Maggie passed but didn't seem to recognize her.

"Where did you go?" Joanie asked, stepping into her path.

"Maggie put both hands on her abdomen. "My stomach."

"I won!" Kimberly said excitedly, coming up beside Joanie and holding up a small trophy shaped like a golden slot machine.

"Great job," Maggie said. "Where's the check?"

"Tonight was just the qualifying rounds. I have to win the next one to win the cash," Kimberly said.

"I came in sixth," Joanie said, "The top ten scores qualify, so I'm in the finals too."

"Great job, girls," Maggie said. "We should celebrate with karaoke."

"You do karaoke?" Kimberly asked, narrowing her eyes.

"No, but I'll watch you girls." Maggie smiled. "I'll tell Mike we'll meet him at the club."

"I'll stop and get David and meet you girls at the Crow's Nest in half an hour," Kimberly said. She held her trophy proudly above her head as she walked out.

"Have you seen John?" Joanie asked.

Maggie stared at Joanie for too long before she answered. "Let's get Mike, and I'll tell you what I saw."

They walked across the room to where the roulette players stood. Maggie motioned to Mike, who saw them. He held up his finger to tell them to wait as the small white ball bounced around and finely settled on a number. It must not have been the right number: Mike shook his head and picked up the remaining chips; then he weaved through the players until he reached Maggie and Joanie.

"How did you ladies do?" he asked.

"Kimberly and I both qualified for the final round," Joanie said. "Kimberly won first place tonight and got a trophy."

"That's awesome. Congratulations, Joanie."

"Not a lot of skill required, brother." She smiled and looked around.

"Where is everyone else?" Mike said.

"Kimberly went to the room to get David. They'll meet us at the Crow's Nest for karaoke."

"What about John?"

"Let's get out of here," Maggie said again. "I'll tell you what I saw."

Maggie motioned them to follow her out into the corridor, where she found a quiet corner with a bench shaped from half of a rowboat. She had them both sit, then she kneeled in front of them and told them how she had followed John and found him with the casino bartender in the business center. "They were leaning over a computer. Then John took something from the printer tray. I couldn't see what it was, but they know each other. They didn't stay long."

"Did they see you?" Mike asked.

"The bartender might have seen me in the hall but didn't seem to recognize me back down in the casino."

"Why didn't you come to get me?"

"You were too far away, and I would have lost track of them. I did what I needed to do."

"Where is John now?" Mike asked.

"I have no idea. I waited for the coast to clear and came back down here."

"Do you think John is our culprit?" Joanie asked the other two.

"He sure is acting suspicious," Maggie said.

"Just because he talks to a bartender doesn't mean anything," Mike said. "He could be asking him for tips on cave diving or something. We shouldn't make out everything as sinister."

"I'll talk to him," Joanie said.

"No, definitely not," Mike said. "Let me and Maggie investigate, and when the time comes, we'll bring you in on it."

Joanie folded her arms across her chest. "Fine, but you need to hurry up. We only have a few days left on this freaking ship. My job is on the line."

"So is Aunt Millie's life savings. We're doing everything we can, Joanie." He put his hand on his sister's. "We're here for you, okay?"

"Fine, just please figure it out—and soon. I'm going crazy, trying to act like everything is normal."

"Let's go join the others, and if I can get away, I'll go look around in John's room and see if I can find the printouts. You two go up to the Crow's Nest, but promise me you won't sing until I get there."

"Don't you worry," Maggie said, "I will not be singing anything tonight—or any night. I don't sing."

"Not even in the shower?"

"Wouldn't you like to know."

Maggie winked at Mike, leaving him standing in place. Maggie followed Joanie but felt Mike watching her as they disappeared around the corner.

Maggie found the gang sitting at one of the front tables. Joanie sat next to Kimberly, who had a large notebook open in front of her, searching for the perfect song. Slips of paper were scattered around the tables. Golf-sized pencils had been set out so would-be singers could write down their selection. David had one of the pieces of paper in his hand as he stood, making his way to the DJ.

The bridesmaids group were gathered on the stage, arranging themselves for their number. They each wore a plastic tiara and pink sashes, indicating their role in the wedding. The maid of honor had control of the microphone. They began singing "We Are Family" by Sister Sledge. Maggie enjoyed watching the dynamics between the girls more than their off-key singing. It was apparent the maid of honor was the dominant personality in the group. Not only did she take center stage, but her movements were also more dramatic, and she almost pushed the others away so she would have more room to work her arms.

Maggie turned her attention to the bride, who was smiling but carried a somewhat sad expression in her eyes. If she could only tell the sweet young girl there were no white picket fences, no magic; but Maggie knew her words would only be wasted.

A few more passengers, all of whom were not half-bad, sang a variety of songs. Maggie was finally feeling relaxed when Mike pulled up a chair and scooted it in next to her. He leaned in close.

"I found the papers they printed out, it was nothing."

Maggie turned toward him. "What is 'nothing'?"

"It was what I thought. A list of rock climbing gear. You know: ropes, harnesses, clips. I think it was inventory from the ship's rock wall."

"You don't think there's anything suspicious about that?"

"I don't. John is a daredevil. He always picks the excursion with the most…you know…He's an adrenaline junkie."

"Well, another dead end, I guess."

Maggie turned as the DJ called David to come up to the stage.

Mike sat back in his chair. "This ought to be good."

The music started, and the group stared in awe as David belted out Sir Mix-A-Lot's, "Baby Got Back."

"This guy surprises me every day," Maggie said to Mike. "If John's not our guy, I'm betting it's this one." She nodded her head toward the stage.

"I don't know. Honestly, I think we're on the wrong track. I'm starting to think none of these people took the money."

"I thought we agreed that the scam wouldn't work without help from inside?" Maggie asked.

"There has to be something we're missing, a key relationship. I wish I knew more about how the system works. 'll talk to my sister tomorrow, but we might have to wait until we get back to investigate at the bank. But, since we're here, we might as well have a little bit of fun." Mike reached across the table and slid the large notebook in front of him.

"You sing?" Maggie asked.

"Only in the shower."

Mike smiled as Maggie raised an eyebrow.

WEDNESDAY

CHAPTER 14

Breakfast Buffet

"Haven't you ever heard of the Ebola virus?" Maggie asked as they exited the elevator on Deck 10.

"You mean coronavirus," Mike said, reaching his hand under the hand sanitizer dispenser. Maggie followed suit, but it wasn't the germs she was afraid of; it was the sea of people they were facing.

"All I know is it's wrong to eat at the buffet on a cruise ship. Look there."

Maggie pointed to an older man who picked up a bagel, put his nose close enough to smell it, then put it back on the pile.

"Don't eat that bagel," was Mike's advice.

"I seriously cannot eat here. Remember, I don't like crowds, and we have a personal chef in our room perfectly willing to make up some eggs Benedict."

"Eggs benedict?"

"Or pancakes, waffles, whatever we want. The poor guy is probably bored to death. We haven't used much of his services since we boarded. He probably thinks we don't like his cooking."

"Seriously, Maggie, I don't think he cares, but we're not here to enjoy ourselves. We have a job to do, and all I know is that John said he was headed to the buffet this morning. In our business, there are times you have to stray out of your comfort zone to get the job done. Well, let me rephrase that. More often than not, our job requires us to stray far from our comfort zone. It's called being adaptable."

"Well, there's our mark." Maggie pointed to the far corner of the vast dining hall.

"Our 'mark'?" He shook his head and smiled as he looked where Maggie was pointing.

"That's him," Mike said, "I wonder who he's sitting with?"

They could only see the back of the man's head, but they could tell he was tall, bald, and wore a ship's crew uniform.

"It looks like the bartender from the casino. I remember I had to do a double take. I saw John talking to him, and I remember thinking they could be brothers. We should go sit by them," Maggie said.

"Good idea." Mike picked up a plate and handed it to Maggie. "Fill this up and meet me at the table behind John, facing the man. Try to blend in."

Maggie took the plate and looked around. A crowd of passengers occupied every square foot of space. To get any food on the plate, she would have to elbow her way into an enormous circular station piled with toast, scrambled eggs, diced potatoes, and what looked like grits. *They must know there are Southerners on board,* she said to herself. There was another circular table piled high with mixed fruit, various types of melon, yogurt, cottage cheese, and granola. She should have made herself stay at that table but watched a kid dip his finger into the strawberry yogurt and put it in his mouth.

"I definitely can't do this," she said aloud but to no one in particular. She looked around and spotted Mike on the other side of the room, next to the waffle station. "Okay, Maggie, buck up," she said, again to no one. She decided to get in line for a spinach-and-mushroom omelet. At least she could watch the cook prepare it. The line wasn't too long, but where she stood was right in front of several grey bins that held silverware tightly wrapped in red cloth napkins. People either said excuse me or reached past her to grab their roll.

At first, a few deep breaths settled her nerves, but the line didn't move, and she felt her body start to shake. She stepped out of the line and bumped into more people. She headed to where the plastic glasses were stacked so she could get some water for her dry mouth.

Unfortunately, this was another popular gathering spot as people continued to reach past her for a glass. Her body began shaking uncontrollably, and her knees were weak. She turned to look for the nearest exit, but tears blurred her vision. Then the world went black.

The next thing she remembered was Mike leaning over her. His blue eyes were full of concern. She was on her back, looking up at him.

"Where am I?" She tried to sit but felt dizzy.

"You passed out," he said. "You also got a pretty good gash in your head."

Maggie reached up to the side of her head and found a huge lump that was painful to the touch. Her hand was sticky; when she looked at it, it was red with blood.

"I told you I had panic attacks," she said.

"Honestly, I thought you were just being dramatic," Mike said. "If it makes you feel any better, I believe you now."

"Gee, thanks, Mike." Maggie smiled but felt like crying. Her head hurt, and she was humiliated. It seemed as if all the hurt she ever felt was bottled up. A crowd formed around her until two crew medics arrived, pushing people aside. They checked her vitals and asked her a few questions that she answered correctly, but they still lifted her onto a gurney then rolled her through a sea of people.

They took her to an unfamiliar hallway. The sound of the crowd faded the farther the medics rolled her. One of the medics continued to check her vitals as they waited for the service elevator. She didn't even feel the cuff going around her arm until it squeezed so tight she thought her arm was going to burst; then it let up. The two medics were both calling numbers out but didn't seem to be too concerned. She quickly wiped the single tear that had escaped the corner of her eye, so Mike, who stood dazed, wouldn't notice.

"Sir, you can meet your wife in the infirmary in a few minutes," one of the medics told him.

She saw Mike's face as the large elevator doors shut. She tried to smile to reassure him, but it just hurt too bad, and her smile became a wince instead.

The medics settled her into a hospital bed in a wide-open space. It looked like an oversized doctor's office. A young brown-skinned woman came to the side of the bed while the medics waited nearby. She was wearing a white officer's uniform with the caduceus stitched on the lapel. "I'm Dr. Rialto," she said smiling, "I heard you had a bit of a fall." She had a beautiful British accent. "Can you tell me your name?"

"Maggie."

"Can you tell me your full name and the year you were born?"

"Margret Anne McFarlin, nineteen sixty-three."

"Okay, good." She smiled.

"Can you tell me what year it is?"

"Twenty twenty?"

"You sound like you're not sure," Dr. Rialto said, concerned.

"No, I'm sure. I'm just not sure why you are asking me all these questions."

"I'm making sure your memory is intact. You may have a concussion, but we'll keep an eye on you for a few hours. I don't want you to sleep. Can you stay awake for me?"

"I guess," Maggie said.

"Well, it's vital that you do. I'm going to keep you here in the infirmary for a few hours to monitor you. You did an excellent job on that head. Does this hurt? She set her fingers to Maggie's face and pressed gently near her eye socket.

Maggie winced. "Yeah, a little."

"It's probably just a bruise," she said then examined the cut on Maggie's head. "I don't think we need to stitch that, but go ahead and seal it," she told one of the medics who had brought her here.

"Seal it?" Maggie said as the doctor walked away.

Dr. Rialto stopped to wash her hands at an oversized sink, using a foot pedal to turn the water on and off. "I'll check on you in a while," she said.

Maggie turned to one of the medics. "What did she mean when she said, 'seal it'?"

The medic smiled. "It's kind of like superglue."

"Gee, I'll bet that's going to be a flattering hairstyle."

"Well, it's a pretty good-sized cut, and the head tends to bleed a lot."

Maggie became busy with the bed controls, trying to find the most comfortable position. She noticed the blood on her brand new shirt just as Mike walked in.

"I brought you this." He handed her a bag marked with the ship's logo. "I decided to buy you a new shirt instead of rifling through your clothes.

Maggie accepted the bag. "You didn't have to do that."

The medic came over to the side of the bed with a rolling tray lined with a white linen covering. The tray held what looked like several medical instruments and a bowl with water and soap. He dabbed Maggie's head with a soapy gauze pad. She winced the first few times he placed the soiled, red-stained pads in a brown paper bag taped to the side of the tray.

Mike, too, winced at the sight of the pads. "Yikes, you okay?"

"I'm fine," she assured him until the medic took a pair of blunt-tipped scissors and clipped her hair.

"Seriously?" Maggie complained.

"Just a bit. I don't want it sticking to the closure."

Maggie rolled her eyes. "Okay." Mike smiled.

"The doctor said you need to stay awake and hang out here for a while," Mike said, sliding a white plastic chair to the side of her bed. "I'll keep you company for a little while."

"You seriously don't need to do that," Maggie said. "You need to stay with the group."

"I'm staying here."

"Well, let's not waste this opportunity, let's go over what we have so far," Maggie said, "even though it's not much."

"Great idea."

Mike pulled a small spiral notebook from his front pocket. It was the same kind that he had used when she first met him. That seemed like years ago rather than months.

"Why don't you just use the Notes app on your phone?"

"I'm an old-fashioned kind of guy, I guess. Plus, I have a system. It works for me."

"Okay, where should we start?"

"David."

"My gut says no," Maggie said.

"Your gut? Okay, but he's so quiet anyway. The quiet ones always have secrets."

"How about Kimberly?"

"Boy, she doesn't like you," Mike said.

"I know. I don't get it. Everyone likes me."

"What's her motivation?" Mike asked, not expecting an answer.

"John is my favorite," Maggie said.

"There's something he's hiding, but he was a marine. Marines have a deep-seated sense of duty and are committed to honesty and loyalty."

"You mean they've been brainwashed during boot camp," Maggie said, gently touching her head and wincing when she did.

"It's not brainwashing. It's a method that works. The drill instructors break you down to build you up," Mike said defensively. "He was Special Forces, that's a whole other personality type: those dudes have to make it through the hell their instructors put them through. If John did it, it was with a more elaborate purpose than simply greed."

"He did spend a lot of cash at the casino," Maggie added. "But he doesn't have access to the computer systems, does he?"

"He's the head of security, so he has access to everything.

He's the first one at work and the last to lock up," Mike said. "Joanie said he works twelve hours a day, five days a week."

"How long has he worked at the bank?" Maggie asked.

Mike flipped through the pages of the small notebook. "Over five years."

"What we are missing is the motivation," Maggie said.

"Money can't be the only motivation," Mike said. "There are plenty of ways to get money other than taking it from an old woman."

"Maybe we should use the scientific method instead of our gut," Maggie said.

"Impressive, Maggie." He held up his little book. "Document. Sort. Analyze."

"It just seems so hard to form a hypothesis until you identify the motive." Maggie pushed a button on her control panel to sit up farther.

"Sometimes, I have four or five hypotheses. The thing is that the guilty party is obvious. It's exactly the person you suspected in the first place. It hardly ever is a mystery, but this one is one of those times, I don't even have a gut feeling. The key to these kinds of cases is to keep an open mind."

"Especially if you know the people involved," Maggie said. "Like your sister."

"My sister?"

"Maybe you're too close to the people involved to have an open mind."

Maggie pushed her legs around and stood up from the hospital bed, feeling a little shaky, her head pounding. She picked up the bag Mike had brought her and opened it to find a bright pink shirt with two green palm trees with a hammock hanging between them. The words *Island Life* were written in script.

Some detective you are, Maggie thought. *I hate pink.*

"Is the size correct?" he said, ignoring her last comment.

"Perfect," she said, measuring each step to the bathroom. She pulled off her white shirt, now stained with blood, careful not to touch her head. She wadded it up and threw it into the trash bin. She pulled the tags off the new T-shirt Mike had given her, not caring if she ripped it. She wouldn't be keeping it.

She pulled the new shirt over her head, again careful not to touch her bump. She looked in the mirror, expecting to be offended by the pink color, but instead she fell back when she saw the stranger in the mirror. Her left eye was bloodshot and a rose-colored patch marked the skin just above her cheek. Dried blood coursed down the side of her face and caked down on to her neck. Her blonde hair stuck to her head where the blood had dried: it was standing straight up where the medic had cut it. Mike had been sitting out there the whole time, acting like everything was normal. *What is wrong with him?*

She came out of the bathroom feeling like Car Crash Barbie.

"You okay?"

Mike stood, sensing a change of mood since she went into the bathroom.

"Do I look okay?" Maggie tipped her head.

"Well, you look like you were run over by a truck, but other than that, the shirt looks great on you."

"Oh, brother," Maggie said. "Where is my phone?"

"Oh yeah." Mike retrieved her phone from his back pocket. "You dropped it when you passed out. I think you might have cracked the screen a little."

Maggie looked at her phone. The crack in the bottom right corner had been there before she passed out, but there was another small cobweb crack on the opposite side.

"Oh well," she shrugged, sitting back on the hospital bed. "Thank you for keeping me company, but honestly, I feel like being alone."

"Are you sure?" Mike stood. Maggie nodded her head. "I completely understand."

Maggie leaned back and pretended to type on her phone while Mike walked out the door. She felt him pause in the doorway, look back, and then close the door softly behind him. She put the phone in her lap and let all her vulnerability wash over her.

She didn't want to feel sorry for herself, but the last bit of control she had walked out the door with Mike. Tears fell uncontrollably. She couldn't push them back any longer. The memory of another life crept into the corners of her brain, threatening to punish her for past sins. She knew if she didn't get control, she might never come back. When she closed her eyes, she saw the bright red stain on the white couch and the memory of examining both wrists, but no cuts, no blood. Relief washed over her, finding the tipped glass and empty bottle of red wine. That was the hardest night of her life. Maggie had been hoping she wouldn't wake up, but when she did, she packed a bag and left Seattle for the last time.

Just as she brushed the tears away with the back of her hand, a slight knock on the door—and the small brunette head peeked in.

"Maggie?"

Joanie moved through the door and gently closed it as if she was sneaking into a place she wasn't supposed to be.

"Hey Joanie." Maggie grabbed a tissue from the table near the bed and blew her nose.

"I came to see how you're doing. I heard you had a bad fall this morning."

Maggie turned toward her. "You can say that."

"Oh, Jesus." Joanie stepped back. "You look horrible."

"It looks worse than I feel."

Joanie sat down in the chair and looked at Maggie with some concern. "Have you been crying?"

"Just a little pity party. My head hurts," Maggie said. "I'm better now."

"That's good."

Joanie leaned back in the chair and put her feet up on the lower rail of the bed.

Maggie felt awkward alone with Joanie. They had never actually been alone without Mike filling in the distance.

"Was Mike here?" Joanie asked.

"He just left," Maggie answered. "I'm surprised you didn't pass him on your way in."

Joanie stayed silent for a long time, looking around the room.

"You don't have to stay here," Maggie said.

"I know," Joanie said.

"So, why are you here?" Maggie decided to ask.

Joanie put her feet back on the floor and turned to face Maggie. "I had another reason to come down here."

"I have to say that's not a surprise," Maggie said.

"I just thought I should tell you I heard Kimberly and David whispering, and I think they may be involved with the scam."

"Why do you say that?"

"They were talking about money and hiding it," she said.

"What specifically, word for word, did they say?"

"I don't know. I was too far away to understand everything. I just know it has to be those two."

"Did you tell your brother?"

"No, I didn't want him to dismiss me. I wanted to tell you."

"Okay, I'll talk to your brother, and we can investigate."

"Good," Joanie said. She stood from her chair and walked out the door, not bothering to close it.

Maggie closed her eyes. That made absolutely no sense, she thought.

CHAPTER 15

Lido Deck

Maggie walked out of the infirmary with Tylenol and a strong warning from the ship's doctor to stay awake for the rest of the day. All other instructions were lost on her as she rushed out and made her way to the suite. The ship was quiet; most of the people had gone ashore for their excursions. She looked forward to a calm day by the pool.

She took a long hot shower, carefully washing the blood out of her hair where she had cracked her skull. She was lucky her injury hadn't required stitches, but the superglue felt like a giant piece of bubblegum stuck to her head. She changed into the tankini she purchased from the Tommy Bahama outlet at the Concord Mall, surprised that it fit fairly well given that she hadn't even bothered to try it on.

The lido deck was desolate. Plenty of deck chairs were available near the adults only pool. She picked a chair in the shade, where she laid out two towels she picked up from the towel kiosk before taking a prone position. She closed her eyes, took a few deep breaths, and let the morning wash away. After she felt her head clear enough to read, she pulled her Kindle out of her bag and flipped through until she found a cozy mystery that looked promising. It seemed like forever since she had read a book for fun. She had been focusing all her spare time studying her online classes for her PI certificate or keeping up on technological changes in her industry just in case she decided to take a job.

After reading the same page three times, Maggie gave up and put on her dark sunglasses. Her head was still pounding, and she couldn't focus. She closed her eyes again, trying not to feel sorry for herself. She heard rustling next to her but didn't bother opening her eyes, but she was curious why someone had to sit next to her when so many chairs were available.

"Are you okay?" said a familiar voice.

Maggie sat up and took her glasses off to find Kimberly on the edge of the lounge chair facing her. Was she dreaming?

"How are you feeling?" Kimberly asked as she began arranging her towel.

"My head is killing me, but I'm more embarrassed that I passed out in front of a room full of people. I heard I took out a small child."

"It wasn't a child. I heard it was an elderly man with a walker." Kimberly smiled.

Now Maggie knew for sure she was dreaming. Kimberly smiled?

"Why aren't you with the group?" Maggie asked Kimberly.

"I don't care to see the sights of Honduras. It's depressing, seeing poverty and suffering. It kills me to see children begging in the streets."

"I don't think they show you those parts."

"Yeah, but you can feel it all around you. Plus, I wanted the time to talk to you."

"Me?"

"Yes. I guess I would like to start with an apology. I feel bad for treating you so poorly."

Maggie tried to sound sincere. "Honestly, I didn't notice."

"I'm not stupid," Kimberly said, "and neither are you."

Maggie turned to face Kimberly. "I never thought you were stupid."

"I know what's going on, and I don't like it."

"You do?" Maggie asked. *Did she*?

"I know Mike is Joanie's brother, and he used to be a detective in Palm Beach County. I know that he runs a detective agency in Salisbury. I know you're not from Corporate. And I know you are investigating me and the others."

"Why do you think we're investigating you?" Maggie asked, looking around for any ears in range, but there were none.

"Last week, my new teller took a deposit from Mildred Brown and deposited it into the wrong account. But when the teller noticed her mistake, she put it back. Unfortunately, she added an extra zero, so the deposit that should have been ten thousand dollars was now $a hundred thousand dollars."

"So, couldn't you just correct that mistake?" Maggie again looked for anyone nearby who might be able to overhear their conversation.

"We could have, but Mildred saw it before I did and withdrew all one hundred thousand dollars."

"Why didn't you tell Joanie?"

"I did. Mildred is her aunt so I figured she would talk to her and get it back, but every time I talk to her about it, she said she would take care of it." Kimberly looked like she was about to cry. "I've been with Brownstone Savings and Loan as long as everyone else, and they are a tight-knit group. Nothing has ever happened like this in my entire career."

"But really, it wasn't your fault. It sounds like the teller's fault," Maggie said, trying to sort out the huge inconsistencies in what Kimberly was saying compared to what Joanie said happened.

"That's the other problem. I let the teller use my login against company policy. It usually takes David several days to issue the individual logins to new employees. We were so busy, and the girl had previous banking experience, so I let her use my login. As far as the bank is concerned, it was me who made a mistake."

"I'm sure the girl will back up your story."

"I tried to call her phone, and the number is disconnected. I even went to the address she provided, and it was the address of the old Cheerwine factory downtown. How can I have been so stupid?"

Kimberly put her hands over her face to hide her anguish. Maggie spotted a poolside server and motioned him over.

"Can we get two Patrón margaritas?" She flashed the card at the end of her lanyard, signaling that the drinks were included with the drink package. Then she turned back to Kimberly. "I'm so sorry,. I have to admit I'm a little surprised you're telling all of this to me."

"I looked you up on the internet. I know you were involved in a murder in Boca Raton." Kimberly took her hands away from her face.

"Technically, I wasn't *involved* in the murder." Maggie deliberately emphasized the word *involved.*

"I needed someone to know my side of the story. I feel like Joanie doesn't believe me when I told her that her aunt was the one who took the money she knew didn't belong to her. Honestly, I feel like Joanie is setting me up."

"Are you one hundred percent sure Mildred deposited the original ten thousand dollars?"

"I guess I'm not one hundred percent sure, but I do remember Mildred being in the bank at the end of the day; but as I said, it was the new girl who did the transactions."

"So, basically, you're asking me to help prove what?"

"I didn't take the money."

She said it almost too loud. The server walked up, tilting his head with interest as he handed Kimberly and Maggie each a plastic margarita glass filled to the brim; the rim of each glass had been thickly salted. Maggie waited for the server to leave before she spoke.

"Do you think someone thinks you did?" She licked some of the salt from the glass then took a sip of the margarita.

"I think Joanie thinks I did it, and I also think she's trying to trick me into admitting I did something I didn't do. Her aunt told her she doesn't have any money, and her aunt's bank account is empty." Kimberly wiped the salt from a section of her glass before she took a long sip.

"So, let me ask you this, who hired the disappearing

teller?" Maggie asked.

"I did, of course, but John highly recommended her. He said he knew her from another bank. Honestly, it's not easy finding someone who will work for low wages in such a regulated industry. I didn't even bother to check her references. I was just happy to have her." Kimberly took another long drink of her margarita; then she signaled the server, who had been standing close by, obviously bored. He started walking toward them, but when Maggie pointed to her glass, he got the signal and turned to get two more drinks.

"I think this is making my head feel better," Maggie said, finishing off her drink, setting the glass down.

"So, are you going to help me figure this out?" Kimberly asked.

"Let me talk to Mike," Maggie started before Kimberly interrupted her with a loud "No!" causing Maggie to jump. "You can't tell him. What if Joanie is responsible somehow. There's no way Mike will turn in his sister. He's been covering for her whole life."

"What do you mean, covering for her?"

"Joanie has been in a lot of trouble in her life. She's far from the Goody Two-shoes she portrays."

"Okay," Maggie said. "I'll keep my eyes and ears open."

"And don't count Joanie out as part of this whole thing."

"Have you spoken to anyone else about this?" Maggie asked. "Like maybe David?"

"Well"—Kimberly hung her head—"a little. I asked him if he could use his security software to trace some other suspicious transactions over the last six months. He said no, and I might have raised my voice a bit."

"Are you two romantically involved?" Maggie asked.

"No, not at all," she said, "but I do trust him, and he could clear me."

Maggie nodded in affirmation but put the thought to the back of her mind; she would evaluate it later. Just then the two margaritas arrived. As she took the glass, someone sat down on the other side of her chair.

Silas.

"What happened to you, Maggie?" Silas whispered loud enough for Kimberly to hear. "You stick your nose in the wrong place?"

"Oh, jeez, what are you doing here?" Maggie asked, ignoring his comments regarding the current state of her face.

"I'm on a cruise," he said, flashing his white teeth. "And who is your beautiful friend?"

"This is Kimberly. Kimberly, this is Silas."

"Very nice to meet you, Kimberly."

Silas stood and moved close enough to Kimberly to hold out his hand. When Kimberly held hers out, he kissed the top of it before releasing it. Kimberly's face flushed as Silas looked her up and down like a hungry hyena.

"Okay, Casanova, we're having a private conversation, if you don't mind," Maggie said. "Why are you on the ship? Shouldn't you be galivanting ashore?"

"Jay and I went on the early dive trip," Silas said, smiling. "We got everything we needed, and now I have a free afternoon to galivant on board."

"What exactly did you *need* on the dive trip?" Maggie asked.

Silas narrowed his eyes. "You know what I mean, sunshine and sharks." He smiled again.

"Sharks?" Kimberly said, surprised.

"We saw a few but didn't get close enough to interact. The ship discourages it."

"Didn't you go on the dive trip when we were in Cozumel?" Maggie asked.

"We did." He smiled. "If you're keeping track, we've taken every dive excursion at every port a dive was offered. Jay and I like to dive."

Maggie rolled her eyes. She looked at Kimberly, who was watching the interaction with too much interest.

"If you girls would like to meet up later for a drink, I'll be at the wine bar at eight o'clock." Silas walked away with his bare chest pushed out to emphasize the body he worked so hard to maintain.

"Who was that?" Kimberly asked.

"No one."

"He didn't look like a no one," Kimberly said.

"Believe me. Silas is not someone you want to know."

"Sounds like you know him pretty well."

"You could say that," Maggie said. Her head was feeling better, but her stomach was hollow: she never had the chance to eat breakfast, and it was already well past lunch time. "Let's go up and see what Chef Paul can throw together for lunch. I missed breakfast."

"Sounds good," Kimberly said. She stood and held out a hand for Maggie, who accepted it. She was beginning to see a whole new side of Kimberly; however, she knew people are tricky. Maggie kept an open mind, but she needed to write down everything Kimberly had told her. She was troubled by the fact that she couldn't talk to Mike about it.

The two women walked side by side, chatting about the ship and their travel companions but nothing beyond the typical surface conversation. When they entered their suite, Ralph came out from the room David and John were sharing. He was holding a small notebook, which he quickly hid in the pocket of his suit. His normally slicked-back hair hung at odd angles, as if he had taken a nap.

"Ladies," he said nervously. "Welcome back. Can I get you a drink?"

Maggie twisted her face and held the drink she carried up from the pool, toward him. "I think we're good," she said. "You okay?"

"Of course." He looked back to the door he just exited. "Just tidying up."

"Is the chef here?" Kimberly asked.

"Of course, let me get him."

Ralph rushed out the sliding glass doors to the balcony. He

quickly closed the doors behind him, watching the women..

"What was that about?" Kimberly asked Maggie.

"I don't know, but whatever it is he's acting guilty of something."

Ralph soon reopened the sliders, letting Chef Paul step in ahead of him.

"Ladies," Chef Paul said.

"We hate to bother you, but would you mind fixing something for lunch?" Maggie asked.

"How about a Chicken Caesar salad?" the chef asked.

"Sounds good to me," Kimberly said.

"Me too," Maggie said, again feeling the rumbles in her empty stomach.

Ralph was still standing at the glass doors. "Why don't you two ladies sit out here with your drinks, and I'll bring your salad as soon as they are prepared."

The two women walked out onto the balcony, but before sitting, they leaned over the rail to take in the view of the Honduran coastline. Maggie looked down. "I wonder what's ' below us?"

"I think it's the bridge," Kimberly said.

"I thought that was on the other side of the ship."

"I believe it takes up the entire deck, from bow to stern," Kimberly said confidently.

Maggie looked wary. "Do you seriously know that?"

"I have no idea. It sounded good, though, right?"

Some of the balconies below had other passengers on them, but most were vacant. They had a great view of the far side of the lido deck, where two ping pong tables stood side by side.

"I would hate to fall overboard from this far up," Kimberly said, leaning toward the rail. "It's a long way down."

"I don't think you would survive," Maggie said, unrolling a blue striped towel and stretching it out on the lounge chair before sitting.

Kimberly stood for a few more minutes at the rail of

the ship, looking down. She shook the rail, which was securely welded; it didn't move. Then Kimberly leaned over as far as she could to get a look at the deck below.

"Don't jump." Ralph stepped out the sliding glass doorway carrying two salads, "Things will get better."

Kimberly turned, smiling. "I was just trying to figure out what was directly below us," she said.

Ralph handed Maggie her salad and set Kimberly's down on a small table. He unrolled her towel and tucked it in the lounge.

"Directly below us is the spa. The next deck above is the back end of the bridge." He handed Kimberly her salad when she settled in her chair. "Now you girls eat, sit back, and relax. You are on vacation. I'll bring the drinks. How does a refreshing mojito sound?"

Both women nodded their heads vigorously as their mouths were full of salad.

CHAPTER 16

Dinner and a Show

John and David were the first to walk into the suite. Both looked as though they had gotten too much sun but were in high spirits. John's bald head was unusually shiny. It looked like a crystal ball ready to predict the future.

"Wow," John said, stopping abruptly in front of Maggie and Kimberly, who were sitting on the couch. "You girls okay?"

Maggie had forgotten this was the first time the guys were seeing her after the incident earlier that morning.

"Can't say it wasn't inevitable," David said casually, looking back and forth between the two women before disappearing into his room. John shook his head and followed David into the bedroom. He looked back to the couch at the two women one more time before shutting the door.

"I guess they can't believe we're getting along," Maggie offered.

Kimberly smiled broadly. "I don't think that's it."

Maggie watched her. It was nice seeing a smile on Kimberly's face. She was such a pretty girl, and when she smiled, her face lit up. Maybe just telling her side of the story had released all the worry she had bottled up.

Moments later, Mike and Joanie walked in and gasped loudly, causing Maggie to stand up.

"What?" Maggie said, looking at the two.

"What happened between you two?" Mike asked.

"We worked it out," Kimberly said. She stood up, tilted

her head and walked into her room, leaving the three alone.

"You okay?" Mike asked, putting his arm around Maggie's shoulder.

"Why is everyone making such a big deal about this? I'm fine. We talked it out. Period."

"Then how did this happen?"

Mike took her hand in his and led her to the entrance of the suite, where a large gold-framed mirror hung on the wall. Maggie looked at her reflection. She didn't recognize the woman looking back at her. A woman with a black eye. It looked like she had been in a fight and she was not the winner. She instinctively put her hand to her face, paying extra attention to her left black eye. She touched it in several spots, but it didn't hurt. It was just black. Her hair was out of control, and with no makeup she was extra pale.

"Wow, it does look bad," Maggie said. "Kimberly never said anything."

"Did she hit you?" Joanie asked from behind her. Maggie turned to face her.

"I didn't hit her," Kimberly said. She had emerged from her bedroom with a strange smile that looked like maybe she wouldn't mind taking the credit.

"No, she didn't hit me," Maggie said. "It's from the fall this morning. But it doesn't hurt."

"Why don't you get in the shower?" Mike turned Maggie toward their shared room. "We can either go to the early seating or eat here, but the show starts at seven. It's supposed to be good."

Maggie took a few steps before she stopped and looked back at Joanie and Mike, who stood frozen, watching her.

"I'm fine," Maggie whispered to herself as she entered the room, closing the door behind her.

*

Maggie let the hot water run over her head and down her body. The bump on her head was still too tender to allow her to scrub out any remaining scabs of blood. She didn't care. Her head was also full of questions. Should she tell Mike what Kimberly said? Was Joanie involved in the scam?

She tied her robe around her waist and went to the closet where Ralph had hung all her clothes. She picked out a short-sleeved teal blouse and white retro bell-bottom jeans. She jumped when she heard a loud snore. Mike was lying on top of his bed, fast asleep. She hadn't noticed him. He was faceup with his mouth wide open.

She walked on her tiptoes as if her bare feet would have made a noise, and stood directly above him. She liked this guy. He had such a good heart, was even-tempered, smart, and attractive. But again, she lived too far away, and she didn't want a causal relationship; she knew a long-distance thing wouldn't work for either one of them. She could hear the voices of her two friends, Britney and Alex, telling her that she was overthinking the whole thing, and she should just go for it.

She turned to get dressed in the bathroom when Mike stirred.

"Hey, you *really* okay?" His hoarse voice sounded concerned.

She turned back to face him. "I'm good."

Mike sat up and patted the bed next to him. "Come sit for a second."

"I'm not as fragile as you think," Maggie said.

"I know that, but I'm concerned. I'm the one who got you into this," Mike said. "I honestly didn't know Kimberly was going to stay behind today. I hope it went okay."

"That was the best part of the day," she said. "We had some one-on-one time and were able to clear the air. I think it's all good now."

"Well, good...Were you able to get any information from her?"

"A little." Maggie hadn't decided whether to share what Kimberly had told her yet. "You need to get in the shower, or we'll be late."

Mike looked at his watch. "Oh yeah. Okay."

He went into the bathroom. As soon as Maggie heard the shower run, she changed into her dinner outfit. She sat on her bed gingerly, picking a brush through her hair, wincing each time she got close to the goose egg on her head.

When Mike finished in the bathroom, she took it over. She dried her hair and put on makeup, but trying to hide her black eye was useless.

She walked into the shared living space, where everyone was sitting around, chatting casually. Ralph handed Maggie a glass of wine.

"You should have seen John." David was speaking directly to Kimberly. "He jumped off that cliff without hesitation."

"Into the water?"

"It was a bungee cord. You get within inches of the water before it snaps you right back up," John said excitedly. "A true adrenaline rush."

"I couldn't do it," Kimberly said.

"Someone would have to push me," Maggie offered. Five heads turned to her, but it was David who said, "It looks like someone already did."

The room broke out in laughter, including Maggie.

*

Maggie's group walked into the dining room. They were greeted by the maître d', who delivered them to a table near the window. The sun was quickly dropping from the sky, providing a magical experience as they took their seats.

Mike held the chair for Maggie. John mirrored the gesture, holding the chair for Joanie, as David did for Kimberly. While the assistant waiter made his way around the table taking drink orders, the head waiter introduced himself as Banyop; his associate was Nyem. "If you can introduce yourselves," he said, "I will not have to ask again."

They each said their names, and Banyop wrote them down on a small pad of paper; but when Maggie's turn came, Banyop's smile turned into shock. He quickly regained his composure.

"Welcome, Maggie"—the assistant came to her side —"what can I get you to drink?"

"I'll have a glass of Cabernet," she said, pointing to the second one on the wine menu. "Hell, bring the whole bottle." She saw the assistant was taking her seriously. "Hey, just kidding. A large glass will do."

He politely smiled as he moved to the others seated at the table. The main waiter gave a rundown of the small menu, complete with his recommendations; but before he finished, John backed his seat away and walked away toward the entrance. The waiter continued as if John hadn't been so rude.

Mike leaned over to Maggie. "What the heck?"

"Wait," Maggie whispered in reply. She pointed under the table to Joanie, who was also backing out from her chair.

"I'll go," Maggie said.

The waiter finally stopped talking and simply smiled and said, "I'll come back in a few minutes to take your order."

As soon as Joanie left her chair, Maggie followed her. Joanie followed John's earlier path and headed out the door of the dining room. Several photographers had set up their stations out on the deck: they were taking pictures of couples as they posed in front of backdrops of sunsets and old barn doors.

Maggie watched Joanie weave around these obstacles until she reached the deck railing, where she leaned over, obviously looking for John. Maggie came up next to her and put her hands on the railing.

"You okay?" Maggie asked.

"I'm fine," Joanie said. "Just needed some air."

"I wonder where John went?" Maggie asked Joanie, who scoured the two levels visible from their vantage point.

The elevator doors opened two decks below them, and there he was. John walked out in his suit and tie. He held the elevator for its other occupants to exit, but there was just one other occupant: Jules, the cruise director, but she wasn't wearing her uniform. Instead, she sported a sapphire-blue full-length gown that sat off her shoulders. Her hair hung in tight curls, falling past her shoulders, instead of being pulled back into a bun. She was striking, with fuchsia-pink lips and enhanced eyelashes.

"What is he doing with her?" Maggie asked innocently.

"That's what I would like to know." Joanie clenched her jaw and stayed tight lipped.

Maggie looked over at Joanie's slanting eyes. "Do you like him?"

Joanie looked back at Maggie and narrowed her eyes even farther. She pushed herself off the railing and turned back to the dining room. She seemed to be walking with purpose. If she stepped down any harder, her heels might drill holes in the carpeting on the deck.

When they returned to the table, they saw that the drinks had already arrived—and Maggie had a full carafe of wine sitting in front of her place setting. She looked at Mike, "I said I was kidding."

"I didn't think he heard you past your black eye," Mike said.

"That makes no sense, Mike. She sat and took a long swallow of the magic grape potion.

"So, what's going on?" Mike asked as Joanie downed her entire Cosmo then motioned the server for another.

"We saw John downstairs with Jules…and Jules was looking hot. I mean *hot,*" Maggie said.

"So do you think…?"

"That's what it looked like, but who knows?" Maggie said.

"Shall I take the orders?" the headwaiter asked.

Mike nodded. "Yeah, let's go ahead. I'm not sure where our friend disappeared to."

Joanie flinched at Mike's words.

John didn't return for the meal. Mike and David kept the ladies entertained with stories from their earlier shore excursions. Joanie remained silent, but with each drink she became more relaxed. The finale was bananas Foster served with a scoop of vanilla ice cream.

No one mentioned John's absence as they made their way to Deck 5, where the theater doors stood open and the audience were taking their seats. John was standing at the door near the elevator. As Maggie and her group approached him, he smiled as if he hadn't left them sitting at the dinner table with no excuses.

"We missed you at dinner," Maggie said.

"You okay?" Mike asked.

"Yeah, yeah, yeah," he said, avoiding the daggers thrown from Joanie's eyes.

"We thought you might have fallen overboard." David punched him in the arm.

"I've fallen all right," John smiled. "We better find a seat." He stood next to the door, letting the group walk in front of them. Kimberly was the first in line: she chose a group of seats still available near the center lower balcony. They filed in behind her. John took the last seat, making sure David was sitting between Joanie and him.

"Awkward," Maggie whispered to Mike.

"I don't know what's going on there, and I probably don't want to know," Mike whispered in return.

"Well, well, well, lookie there."

Maggie pointed to the stage. Jules was walking to the center, followed by a spotlight. She looked even more glamourous than she had earlier. Her dress danced lustrously as the spotlight reflected off the sequins woven into the shiny blue fabric.

"Ow," Mike said, looking over at Joanie's blank stare as she looked forward without a flinch.

"Welcome to an exceptional production tonight," Jules announced into the microphone. "Is there anyone here from Las Vegas?"

A small group sitting somewhere on the second level of the balcony erupted in cheers.

"Well, this is not Vegas." A spattering of people laughed, not sure where Jules was going. "It's better." The crowd erupted with cheers. "Please sit back and enjoy the ship's production of *Circuit Olé.*"

She waved her arm, and the curtain rose as she disappeared over to the side stage.

The production was a hilarious spoof of Vegas' famous Cirque du Soleil. In this production, a group of Hispanic dancers arrived at an open call in Vegas for the legendary production only to be rejected by the producers. They decide to form their own team of dancers and design a show, which was a total flop, but the audience roared with laughter as the actors attempted the complicated acrobatics. Maggie laughed so much her stomach hurt more than her head.

The group dispersed after the show. Maggie and Mike decided to try the brew pub before retiring for the night. Maggie was eager to spend time with her informal partner. As they walked past the shops and the pizzeria, she endured continual side glances from the other passengers who were walking by, and she even heard an older woman comment, *"He should be ashamed of himself!"*

"Why do some people instantly go there?" Maggie asked.

"Go where?" Mike asked. He pointed at the brew pub across the way. They wove their way through the stands selling watches, perfumes, gold by the inch. The brew pub's wood-paneled façade with large barrels set up as tables led to a cozy little bar.

A young man with a guitar strummed a soulful tune. He read the song's lyrics from a small screen on a stand in front of him. He looked up to greet the pair but flinched when he saw Maggie's face. He quickly recovered and continued to sing.

"I must look horrible," Maggie said as she sat down. "All night, people have had a shocked look on their face when they see me."

"You look beautiful," Mike told her. "It's just the black eye is a little distracting."

"I finally stopped looking in the mirror," Maggie said. "I look like a fighter in the M-M-A."

"It will be better tomorrow," Mike replied, smiling, "or next week. Honestly, Maggie, you are a beautiful woman, inside and out."

Maggie smiled. "Thank you, Mike. I meant to tell you how extremely handsome you look this evening."

Mike smiled too, and Maggie saw the sparkle that drove her crazy shining in those blue eyes.

But just as they might have shared a moment together, all hell broke loose.

CHAPTER 17

Man Overboard

"Oscar-Oscar-Oscar!"

A loud disembodied voice came over the loudspeaker. Maggie felt the ship go quiet. She didn't even notice the silence of the engines.

"What's going on?" she said aloud.

"Something serious," Mike answered, standing.

"Oscar-Oscar-Oscar!" the voice again called. Several crew members ran aft.

Again the voice announced *"Oscar-Oscar-Oscar!"* but this time followed it with two critical words: *"Man Overboard!"*

"Oh, my God." Maggie stood. "How could someone fall off the boat?"

"Probably drunk," Mike said. "Let's go up into the suite and see if we can see anything from our balcony."

As they made their way to the elevators, they saw more ship personnel running aft or speaking into walkie talkies. At least the commotion took the other passengers' attention away from her face. She was sure people assumed she was a victim of domestic violence.

The tumult on the deck below was eerily quiet while the elevator slowly rose to Deck 11. Still, as soon as the doors opened to the ordinarily quiet corridor, Mike and Maggie found it was full of uniformed bodies. A large man stood in front of the door.

"That's our suite," Mike said, pointing to the door behind

the man.

"You can't go in," the man said firmly. He moved to block the door further.

"My sister is in there. You're not going to stop me!" Mike said determinedly.

"Fine, just wait here for a moment." The big man fished a key card from his pocket. As soon as the door clicked, he opened it with a warning: "Just wait here."

Mike and Maggie waited. It wasn't long before the man came back and held the door open for Mike and Maggie. "Go ahead," he said, then closed the door behind them.

Mike and Maggie walked into the shared living space and saw Joanie standing with her hands behind her back. Randolph stood next to her.

"What's going on?" Mike asked.

Joanie turned, revealing silver handcuffs around her wrists. "I'm under arrest." Her words were slurred with intoxication.

"You can be under arrest on a ship?" Maggie asked.

"It appears that Ms. Brown pushed Mr. Haas off the balcony," Randolph said.

"I didn't push him..."Joanie started. "Well, I did push him but not over the balcony. John was drunk, and he was saying some inappropriate things. I left him on the deck over there." She gestured with her head, indicating the left side of the balcony, where the hot tub sat.

"Joanie— Mike looked at her—"don't say another word, okay?"

She nodded her head, slowly trying to follow Mike's gestures.

Mike looked at Randolph quizzically. "Are there any cameras?"

"Unfortunately, there aren't cameras by the hot tub. It's considered a privacy zone. Cameras on several of the other decks might have caught the fall. I'll make sure we check every angle," Randolph said. "I'm sorry, but I'm going to have to hold her until we dock, when the authorities can take over."

"How long is that?" Mike asked.

"I can't say," Randolph said solemnly.

"This is ridiculous, look at the size of her, John is so much stronger than her," Mike said with authority.

"We have two eyewitnesses that say different. Again, I'm sorry, I'll let the authorities handle it," Randolph said pointing to David and Kimberly at the same time taking Joanie's arm.

"Technically, they aren't exactly 'eyewitnesses' if they didn't see her push him over," Maggie said.

"You okay?" Mike asked Joanie as Randolph guided her past him.

"I'm fine," she said sternly. "Just please figure this out and get me off this ship."

"I will," he said as he followed her to the door. "I'm coming with you," he added.

Randolph turned back. "Why don't you all just get a good night's sleep. I promise there will be no interviews with Ms. Brown tonight. I'm sure she will go right to sleep."

"I'm not going to get any sleep in a jail cell," Joanie said.

Randolph faced Mike, whose face had gone pale. "I could call the locals, but we're not under United States' jurisdiction, so local laws would govern the investigation, trial, and punishment—or I can hold her until we get to Florida."

"We'll wait." Mike said. He looked at his sister.

"I'll be fine," Joanie said with strength.

"We'll take good care of her, I promise," Randolph said.

Maggie put her hand on Mike's forearm. "She said she would be fine."

Randolph led Joanie out of the suite and down the corridor. The large man who had been stationed in front of the door followed close behind.

"I can't believe this is happening," Maggie said. She watched as two of the ship's crewmen fastened a chain through the handles of the door out to the balcony so that no one could go outside. One of the crewmen installed a lock on the chain, to protect any evidence.

"Something's not right. John didn't seem like he was drinking, and Joanie was drunk. I don't see how she could have overpowered him physically." Mike seemed to be talking to himself. "It sure would help if I got a look at the other side of that ledge. If I remember correctly, there's a pretty high railing. She would have to lift him over."

"Let's go look out our room balcony and see if there's anything obvious from there," Maggie said.

"Not until I talk to these two," Mike said, pointing to David and Kimberly, who had been sitting on the couch silently watching the drama unfold in front of them.

Mike sat on a chair facing them, wringing his hands.

"She did it," Kim volunteered.

David pointed to the barstools at the overhang into the kitchen. "We were standing right there."

"We heard Joanie screaming at him," Kimberly said.

"What was she saying?" Mike asked.

"They shut the door so that we couldn't hear everything, but she was mad. Joanie had her finger in John's chest. He was backing up until they disappeared behind the hot tub. The next thing we knew, he was gone."

"Overboard," David said.

"Apparently." Mike leaned forward. "So you didn't actually see John go overboard or Joanie push him? Tell me exactly what happened?"

"Why are you so interested? You sound like a cop," David said.

"He is a cop—"Kimberly sat back, folding her arms in front of her—"or *was* a cop."

Mike looked back at Maggie, who shook her head and lifted her shoulders.

"She didn't tell me," Kimberly said, "but like I told her, I'm not stupid. I knew you were Joanie's brother from the beginning."

"You're Joanie's brother?" David furrowed his eyebrows.

"And you work at Corporate? *And* you're a cop? I am so confused."

"He was a cop. He's a private investigator now—and he *is* Joanie's brother," Kimberly said again. She turned to face David before turning again to Mike. "I graduated with Joanie. I remember you very well. You bailed that girl out of trouble many times, but this time, I don't think you can get her off of murder charges."

"Are you Joanie's sister?" David asked Maggie.

"For such a smart guy, you're such an idiot," Kimberly said. She stood. "I'm out of here. Night-night all."

"I can't believe Joanie killed John," David said after Kimberly had left. He shook his head. "They were such good friends."

"She didn't kill him," Mike said confidently. "David, did you hear anything that was said out there? Anything at all?"

"I didn't hear the words, just Joanie screaming, and John wasn't saying anything, or if he did, it was too low for us to hear. The only thing I thought was weird was I heard John laughing. The next thing we knew, Joanie came in panicking, saying John jumped off the boat."

"She said he jumped?" Mike asked.

"That is exactly what she said."

"Who called for help?"

"Ralph called Randolph."

"Where is Ralph now?" Mike asked, looking around.

"I don't know. He disappeared when Randolph got here."

Mike ran into his bedroom then came out with the card Ralph had given them the first day they arrived. He went to the house phone and punched in a few numbers.

"Hey, it's Mike." Mike spoke into the phone for a few moments then hung up. "He's on his way."

When Ralph walked in, he was visibly upset. He ran his hands through his hair several times, leaving it sticking out at all angles. His face was pale.

"You okay? Ralph," Mike asked.

"Do you need a drink?" Maggie said.

Ralph nodded. Maggie went over to the shelf of liquor and picked out the tequila. She brought over the bottle and a shot glass. Ralph reached over and took the shot. Then he sat down on the couch.

"Did you see what happened?" Mike asked Ralph.

"I was putting glasses in the dishwasher when Ms. Brown and Mr. Haas came in the door. They were arguing about something."

"Did you catch what they were arguing about?"

"No, I stayed unseen in the kitchen."

"So, you didn't catch anything?"

"No. Well, I heard something about Jules, but I didn't understand."

"Then what happened?" Mike asked.

"When David and Kimberly came in, Joanie and John went out to the balcony and closed the door." Ralph looked toward David for confirmation.

"They were standing right there." David pointed to the space where the two large doors came together. "Kimberly and I just sat on the couch. I saw Joanie poking him in the chest. It looked like he was smiling, but she was backing him up with every poke until they disappeared behind the hot tub over there, and we couldn't see them anymore. But we could still hear them."

Ralph reached across and grabbed the tequila bottle; he poured himself another shot. He held the bottle toward Maggie, who shook her head. "Wine and tequila, not a good mix," she said. Mike also shook his head.

"Did you see Joanie push Mike off the balcony?" Mike asked, silently pleading for some detail that would save his sister.

"No. Like I said, I was trying to mind my business in the kitchen. When Joanie came in, she was yelling, '*He jumped!*' That's when I called security."

"What did Joanie do next?" Mike asked.

"She just sat there." Ralph pointed to the chair where Mike

was now sitting.

"Like nothing happened?" Maggie asked.

"She seemed calm. Maybe in shock," David suggested. "She didn't talk until Randolph came in and said the whole...'You have the right to...' blah...blah...blah."

"Miranda," Maggie said, remembering her online lessons. The Fifth Amendment...ensuring a person's right not to incriminate themselves.

"Did she say anything to Randolph?" Mike asked, ignoring Maggie.

"Yeah," David said. "She said *he jumped.*"

"Anything else?" Mike asked.

"She said she would wait for her brother. Which didn't make sense at the time, since I had no idea that you are her brother."

Ralph looked at Mike. "You're Joanie's brother?"

"It's a long story," Maggie said.

Ralph stood from the couch. "Do you have any more questions for me?" he asked Mike.

Mike shook his head. "No, thanks, Ralph. Have a good night."

Ralph took the tequila bottle from the table where Maggie had left it. He still held the shot glass in his other hand. "Goodnight all," he said as he walked out the door.

"Why would he jump?" Mike asked aloud, but he was talking to himself. He loosened his bow tie, having a difficult time with it until it finally came free. He threw it across the room.

"Well, I doubt if he committed suicide," Maggie said. She suffered a barely disguised scowl from Mike.

"If he's dead, he jumped himself, or it was just a horrible accident," Mike said, "but one thing's for sure, my sister isn't a murderer."

"We should at least take her something to wear," Maggie said.

"Good idea. I won't be able to sleep without talking to my sister," Mike said.

Kimberly must have heard their conversation, because just as Maggie approached the room, the door flew open, and Kimberly handed her a small pile of clothes. She had changed, but not into her pajamas. She was wearing a pair of white shorts and a loose blue top over the top of a bathing suit, her hair curled, and she had put on fresh makeup.

"Where are you going?" Maggie asked.

"Wine bar."

Kimberly smiled. Maggie looked at her watch. A quarter to eight.

"Kimberly, I don't think that's a good idea," Maggie said.

"You know what a good idea is? That you mind your own business."

Kimberly brushed past Maggie and left the suite without looking back.

"We can't go down there now," Mike said. He had been talking on the house phone, which he now hung up.

"Can we at least get her a change of clothes?"

"It will have to wait until morning," Mike said, sitting slowly on the couch. "She doesn't want to see us until morning."

"She'll be okay," Maggie said, sitting on the coffee table to face him.

"She *didn't* kill John. I don't know what happened on that deck, but I'm one hundred percent sure she did not push him over."

Maggie placed a hand on his knee. "It might have been an accident."

"No." Mike shook his head. "Something's not right."

Maggie didn't know what to say to comfort him, so she remained silent.

"I'm going to take a shower and go to bed." Mike stood and left the room.

Maggie looked at her watch. It was too early for bed. She considered walking down to the wine bar to see what Kimberly and Silas were doing, but instead, she took a bottle of Cabernet and headed for the business center, where she could use a computer.

THURSDAY

CHAPTER 18

The Brig

Mike and Maggie located the ship's brig on Deck 1. It was just a few doors past the infirmary where Maggie had found herself the morning before. As soon as they entered they found a tired young woman sitting at a metal desk. She lit up as they approached but couldn't hide the dark circles under her eyes. She must have worked the night shift, and her shift would be ending soon.

"We're here to see Joanie Brown," Mike said.

The woman looked at the computer screen and yawned. "The woman they brought in last night?"

"That would be her," Mike said.

The woman, whose name tag just said *Sally*, looked them over and picked up the phone in front of her. She pressed a few buttons. "There are two people here to see the Brown woman," Sally said into the receiver. She looked Mike and Maggie up and down as if someone was describing them on the other end. "Yeah, that's them…Okay…Later." She hung up the phone and said, "You can go in." She pointed to the gate behind her and pushed a button. The gate clicked loudly, and Mike pushed on the metal until the latch released. He stood aside and let Maggie in. The gate closed behind them with another loud click. The small hallway opened into a space divided by thick metal grates. Surprisingly there were portholes in both of the two cells, providing detainees a view of what they were missing.

Joanie was leaning against the dirty white bulkhead as

she sat on a simple cot covered by a tight white sheet, a thin pillow, and an olive-green blanket. She was still wearing her formal black gown from the night before but had gathered it up around her legs. Her formal hairdo was loose. She brushed the long brown strands out of her face then casually waved as they entered. She didn't appear too distraught.

"You think there's a need for two jail cells on a cruise ship?" Maggie asked as she approached the cell where Joanie sat locked up.

"I would imagine that these cells normally hold drunks. They probably have two cells, so drunks can be separated if they're not getting along," Mike said.

"Occasionally, we lock someone up for petty theft or bringing contraband on board," Randolph added, causing Maggie to jump.

"I didn't hear the gate open," Mike said.

"I came in the back door." Randolph pointed behind him. Maggie looked around then noticed the door. She also saw cameras in each corner of the room, their lenses aimed at the cells.

"It smells like puke and Lysol in here," Joanie complained. She stayed in her position against the wall, drawing her knees to her chest.

"Yeah, that's a regular occurrence in these cells," Randolph said. Then he leaned back toward the door Maggie and Mike had entered from and yelled, "Sally, can you bring two chairs?"

Sally appeared, dragging two plastic chairs. She left them just inside the doorway. Randolph handed one of the chairs to Mike, who passed it to Maggie, who set it in front of the bars to Joanie's cell. Mike set the second chair next to Maggie, who was already sitting down.

"Can I talk to you for a second?" Randolph motioned Mike to come with him back out the door. Maggie sat, looking at Joanie, who just remained silent. When Mike came back in, he sat, folding his hands nervously.

"Where did your friend go?" Maggie asked.

"He's giving us some private time," Mike said.

"Not too private."

Maggie pointed to the cameras. Mike nodded his head in acknowledgment.

"They're still searching for the body," he said.

Joanie moved to the end of the mattress as if she could hear better a few inches closer.

"The body?" Joanie asked. "He might still be alive?"

"There's no way he could have survived the fall from that high up. But what I don't understand is how you could have pushed him over the rail. It's pretty high," Mike said.

"I didn't push him over," Joanie said, suddenly standing barefoot at the bars.

"The ship has been stationary since the incident, and there are two more ships in the area searching for John's body," Mike said.

"I *didn't* push him overboard," Joanie said again.

"We don't think you did." Maggie looked at Mike, who remained silent.

Maggie pulled out her phone and clicked on the Notes app. "Can you tell us what exactly happened?"

"We were having a drink. John suggested we do a shot. I said no. I was already drinking wine and didn't want to get sick. John didn't take no for an answer and brought us both shots anyway. It was pretty good, and he handed me another one. I noticed John wasn't drinking as much. I think he had a beer or something. I just figured he was trying to get me drunk, but I wasn't. I was a little tipsy when we went outside to the deck. I figured he was going to make a move, but he didn't. He started saying some ridiculous shit that didn't make sense. He said he knew what I did, and he could prove it. I said I didn't do anything. He said he had proof."

"Proof of what?" Maggie asked as Mike listened stone-faced.

"He was smiling the whole time. I finally told him I knew he had something to do with the scam. He said, 'Prove it.' I had just said it hoping he would admit something. He said it was all my fault and that there's plenty of evidence against me. He showed me a notebook with notes that I had made—notes with account numbers. He said money was missing from all those accounts. He said he was going to go straight to the bank president when we got back home. I was just trying to get the notebook out of his hands."

"What notebook?" Mike asked.

"It was a small spiral notebook. I brought it with me because I couldn't leave it on my desk at work and didn't want the kids to come across it at home."

"Why on earth would you have account numbers written down in a notebook?" Mike asked, shaking his head lightly.

"It was for something I was working on. Don't worry, Mike. I promise it's nothing illegal."

Maggie set her chin in her hand. "What color was the notebook?" she asked..

"Red, why?" Joanie asked.

"I saw Ralph coming out of the guys' bedroom with a small spiral notebook. He didn't expect me to be there, and he slipped it into his pocket."

"Ralph?" Mike looked at Maggie. "The butler guy?"

"Yeah, Ralph, he looked pretty surprised when he saw me and Kimberly come in the door. I guess he thought we had gone on the shore excursion. His hair was messy, and he was carrying a notebook."

"A red notebook?" Mike asked. "It wasn't necessarily the same notebook."

"You're the one who doesn't believe in coincidences," Maggie said to Mike.

"Well, how did it get from Ralph to John?" Joanie said.

"He was coming out of the room not going in," Maggie added.

"My notebook is in the front pocket of my suitcase," Joanie said. "You can check if it's still there.".

"It doesn't make sense, Joanie," Mike said.

"Fine," Joanie said. "It wasn't bank accounts, it was information on my kids. The two babies I gave up for adoption. I keep track of them, and I use resources from the bank to keep track of them. I can't just leave that information lying around at home, so I brought it with me."

"Oh no, Joanie, you didn't."

"Whatever, Mike. It's my business, but what we need to figure out right now is why John jumped. You need to get me out of here."

Joanie sat back on the metal bed, causing it to squeak loudly.

"Is there anything you can think of that you haven't told us already?" Mike asked his sister.

"There is one thing I didn't mention that might be important." Joanie hung her head. Maggie and Mike waited silently for the next words. "I was sleeping with him."

"*What?*" they both said at the same time.

"You slept with John?" Mike said, leaning forward.

"You say that like it's such a bad thing," she said.

"It is a bad thing. You just got out of a bad relationship. You are *always* just getting out of a bad relationship. That's just not how you fix things, Joanie. Why don't you give yourself a break." Mike's tirade started as anger but ended with sorrow: his last words were barely a whisper.

But Mike's distress unraveled Joanie. She came close to the bars to spit her objection: "You are not and never will be my judge, big brother. Do you know why you think you are so much better than me, Michael? Because you had a narcissistic father whose big achievement in life was to have a son and a helpless mother who depended on her son to take care of her because her husband sure didn't."

Mike moved to leave but froze. He looked back with tears in his eyes, but it didn't stop her. "Don't worry about me. I can take care of myself. Like I always have and always will. Why don't you just go play house with this Boca chic." She turned, giving Maggie a chance to escape behind Mike.

"Jesus, Joanie. We're trying to help you out here. The world doesn't revolve around you. Other people have feelings. Your pity party isn't helping anyone, and I've been there for you every single time you needed me. Lots of people in the world have mommies who don't love them enough. I wish for once in your life you could care about someone other than yourself."

"I'm the one going to prison, Mike. For something I didn't do." Tears ran from Joanie's eyes. She put her face into the pillow.

"You're not going to prison." Mike's voice was too low for Joanie to hear, but Maggie heard him loud and clear. Joanie's brother was going to do everything in his power to help his sister.

The two walked silently down the corridor. Maggie watched Mike wipe tears from his eyes even as he remained silent. She followed him, evaluating the brother-and-sister dynamic that had just played out in front of her.

Mike continued to walk silently down two corridors, almost as if he was lost.

"Where was that computer room?" Mike asked her.

"Deck Seven," she said.

"I need to check on something. I'll meet up with you later."

"Are you sure?" Maggie asked.

"I'm sure," Mike said as he punched the button on the elevator door. They both rode silently. The door opened at Deck 7, and Mike stepped out. He didn't look back. Maggie continued back to the suite, where she spent the rest of the day relaxing. Eventually, when she grew hungry and Mike had still not returned, she decided to try to find him.

She found him. He was still in the business center, eyes glued to a computer screen.

"You okay?" she asked.

"Yeah, I'm good." He sat back, stretching his back, raising his arms above his head.

"Have you eaten anything today?"

"Randolph brought me lunch earlier."

"Randolph?"

"Yeah, he's helping me sort out a few things." He pressed a few buttons on the keyboard then stood up.

"Are you ready to go to dinner?" Maggie asked.

"What I *really* need is a drink," Mike said, tucking his little spiral notebook into his front pocket.

Maggie followed Mike, who was once again lost in his thoughts until they reached Keys. It was a piano bar and the first place they came across that served food.

"This looks nice and quiet," he said, motioning Maggie to follow. Several couples were enjoying drinks at small tables covered in red linens. The music was soft, muted by heavy curtains and large paintings that covered the walls. The pianist smiled as his fingers marched across the keys while Mike and Maggie walked by. A tip jar held just a few bills, indicating the start of the pianist's shift.

Candles on the tables flickered, affording the bar a romantic atmosphere, but they weren't there for romance. They sat at the table farthest from the entrance, near a large window. The ship was still at a standstill while the search for John's body continued in full force. Earlier announcements indicated they would remain stationary for a while, but the passengers should continue to go about their activities.

Mike ordered two martinis, not even bothering to ask Maggie her preference. His face was slack, without emotion.

Maggie picked up the small candle from the center of the table. She turned it in her hand, fascinated. "This is real wax but it's a fake flame. It looks so real from afar."

No reaction from Mike. He still just stared straight ahead.

Maggie looked around for another distraction but found none. She wanted to say something but couldn't. The awkwardness continued until the drinks arrived. Mike drank his down in one long swallow, emptying the glass before the server even left the table. He signaled the server for two more, not even noticing Maggie's tentative sip; she gave a one-eyed wince in response to Mike's order. She wasn't a drinker of traditional martinis.

Maggie preferred to mask the alcohol with some food. She slid her glass to Mike, who, without questioning her, drank it down. When the server delivered the next set of martinis, Maggie asked for a Cosmopolitan. She also ordered the first few appetizers from the small menu in front of her. The waiter reached for the drink he'd set in front of her, but Mike waved him away. After the second drink, he slowed down, and Maggie could see his shoulders relax.

"I'm sorry about my sister," he finally spoke.

"You don't have to apologize. Every family has issues."

Maggie considered whether to tell Mike about Kimberly's suspicions about Joanie but decided it still wasn't the right time. She chose to focus on the internal conflicts he was trying to deal with at the moment.

"Do you want to talk about it?" she said, putting her hand on his arm. He looked up, meeting her eyes. She could see sadness but recognized the strength still there.

"Joanie has had a hard life," he started, "and she was right about our parents. Our mother didn't want children, but my father insisted. 'Need to continue the family name,' he said—and sure enough, I was born."

"I'm surprised you aren't a 'junior,'" she said.

"I am. I just don't use the designation." Mike took another sip from the martini. "My parents were almost forty when they had me, and when my mother was pregnant with Joanie, I was already in kindergarten. My mother was so distraught she barely got out of bed her whole pregnancy; when Joanie was born, my mother hardly took care of her. It was Aunt Millie, my father's sister, who took over. She even bought the house next door so she could be there for Joanie. Honestly, I look back on the whole ordeal and wonder why they didn't give her up for adoption. I guess they might have if not for Aunt Millie."

"That's horrible," Maggie said.

"Honestly, it wasn't as bad as it sounds. My father did a

great job providing for his family, but in my parents' eyes, I could do no wrong, and they blamed Joanie for everything that went wrong. You would think that I would be okay with that, but I wasn't. I carried the guilt for my sister; that, and the pressure to achieve and keep my parents happy, was intense. The one person who understood was, again, Aunt Millie."

"She seems like a wonderful woman," Maggie said.

"I think her childhood was much like ours, but she doesn't seem to hold the resentment like Joanie," Mike said. The alcohol was doing its job, and Mike was now sufficiently relaxed.

"Don't get me wrong, Maggie, she's a great girl with a good heart. She just can't help herself sometimes. I think she's just looking for that unconditional love that just doesn't exist."

"You don't believe in love?" Maggie asked.

"My definition of love is probably much different than yours," he said.

"Go ahead, now I'm curious. What is your definition of love?"

"First of all, the word 'love' is just that. It's just a word. When people say they are in love, they're describing the chemical phenylethylamine, which causes dopamine, serotonin, and oxytocin to be released into their brain; that stimulates the need to procreate."

"Seriously, Mike? Is that your belief?"

"That is exactly my belief. Love is just a word. Have you ever been in love?"

"I believe I was once," Maggie said softly.

"But where is he now?" Mike asked. "It was a temporary feeling, and it's over now, right?"

No, it's not right, Maggie thought but stopped short before feeling sorry for herself.

Mike finally told her what he had found in his research that day. Maggie listened closely. They now had a new suspect, one who wasn't on the cruise. Joanie's old boyfriend was out of jail, and Joanie had been in touch with him.

"But how would he have the kind of access he'd need to

pull off the scam?" Maggie asked.

"He's a very resourceful guy," Mike said.

Maggie yawned and looked at her watch. It was a little past midnight.

"Do you '*love*' chocolate?" she asked Mike.

"I do," he said, tilting his head. "You know, phenylethylamine is also stimulated by chocolate."

"Well, follow me, Alex Trebek."

She stood, holding out her hand.

CHAPTER 19

The Chocolate Fountain

Every night at midnight, the ship provided the most spectacular dessert stations, complete with a five foot tall chocolate fountain. The elevator opened at Deck 10. The first station was a table of chocolate martinis and a variety of other cordials. The night sky was clear; a soft breeze carried the fragrances of freshly baked goods. Tables had been set up with every imaginable dessert surrounding the giant fountain.

"I think that's a lot of *feminine*—or whatever chemical you were talking about," Maggie said, smiling.

"Phenylethylamine," Mike said.

"Whatever," she said, "let's get happy,"

They both filled their small plates to the brink, piling up a variety of sweets before settling at a small table overlooking the water. Their conversation took on a less severe tone as they argued over what the best dessert was.

"When we get back, I'm going to make you a Cheerwine float," Mike said. "It's the best thing you ever tasted. The key is the old-fashioned vanilla ice—"

He stopped midsentence and pointed. David and Kimberly had their arms around each other.

Maggie leaned back. "Not as big of a deal as you think."

"I admit, I didn't see that coming," Mike said. "I guess this is the Love Boat, after all. First Joanie and John, and now David and Kimberly. We're the only ones sharing a room, and there's nothing between us."

Maggie swallowed hard, putting her plate down. "So, there is *nothing* between us?"

Mike's face changed as he looked at her. "No, I didn't mean it like that. I like you…"

"Please stop, Mike. I am not asking for *something* to be there. I just felt a little something, but I didn't want—"

Mike leaned forward and put his lips on Maggie's. He kissed her softly at first, and when she responded, he kissed her harder, putting his hand behind her head.

"I knew it!"

Kimberly stood above them, her hands on her hips. David was beside her.

Thanks a lot, Maggie thought.

"You two are ridiculous." Kimberly narrowed her eyes.

"It's none of your business, Kimberly. Maggie stood and then added, "How's Silas?"

"If you want to know, ask him. He's standing right over there."

Kimberly pointed behind Maggie. Maggie turned slowly and saw Silas and Jay leaning against the bulkhead. Silas held his beer up and nodded his head in acknowledgment. She was suddenly humiliated. He had evidently watched the entire interaction between her and Mike, including the kiss.

"I'll be right back."

Maggie marched over to where the two men stood. Kimberly watched her. "This ought to be good," she said, sitting in one of the empty chairs at the table. She motioned for David, who was confused. He took a seat next to her.

"Who is that?" Mike asked Kimberly.

"You know, I'm not exactly sure, but what I do know is those two have history."

Maggie faced Silas and whispered loudly: "What are you guys doing here? Are you spying on me?"

"We aren't spying on you," Jay said. "We were just as surprised to see you on this ship as you were surprised to see us."

"Just a lucky coincidence," Silas said with a wink of his

eye.

"We're actually on the job," Jay said. "Remember?"

"Alex said she didn't know you were here," Maggie said.

"We have more than one client, Maggie," Silas reminded her, "and according to your friend over there, you might need some help on your big case."

"We don't need your help, but thanks for the offer," Maggie said, looking back toward her table. Mike was at full attention, watching her.

"How much did Kimberly tell you?"

"She thinks she's the object of a setup and that her boy toy over there is going to help her prove it."

"David?"

"If he's the I-T guy, then yeah, David," Silas said.

"I can't believe she told you all that."

"What can I say, Maggie, I have a way with women." Silas reached out, but Maggie took a step back, out of his reach. She was uncomfortable with how he was looking at her. She turned and saw that Mike, Kimberly, and David were watching them.

Silas smiled. "Oh, sorry, I don't want to upset the apple cart?"

"What the heck does that mean?" Maggie said.

"It looks like you got something going on over there, I don't want to make the guy jealous."

"Oh, brother." Maggie shook her head, "Maybe it's not a good idea that you guys interact with Kimberly. She could be the one who took the money."

"I think the boss lady did it," Silas said. He finished his beer and tossed it into a nearby garbage can. He motioned to an attendant, who almost instantly brought him a new one.

"Why would Joanie steal from her aunt and her bank?" Maggie asked not expecting an answer.

"Hmm, she hired her brother and his girlfriend. I'm pretty sure she's smarter than you're giving her credit for," Silas said. "Don't be so naïve, Maggie, money does strange things to people. It negates things like decency and breaks family ties. Haven't you ever seen what happens when grandma dies. The family goes to war over a Hummel figurine because it's worth a hundred bucks."

"I guess you're right. But I just don't see it being Joanie," Maggie said.

"You know I will always have your back, Maggie."

"Thanks, Silas, I appreciate it."

A Beach Boys tribute band called the Sandy Sons started to play across the deck from the chocolate fountain. The loud music made it a bit more challenging to carry on a conversation, but the band sounded good.

"I've got to go," Maggie said. Turning, she almost ran into Mike, who had left his chair.

"Let's dance," he said, checking out Silas and Jay up close.

"Okay."

Maggie took his hand, sensing the testosterone pulsing through Mike's veins. She pulled him to the center of the deck where the crowd had started to dance.

Mike was a little wobbly on his feet. He had consumed a lot of alcohol, and it was starting to show. He took Maggie by the hand and slow danced to "Good Vibrations" while the rest of the dance floor was doing the twist, the grasshopper, or whatever dance they were doing. A few crashes into other couples encouraged Maggie to get Mike back in his seat. He seemed perfectly content with letting her lead him around, so she slowly danced to the edge of the dance floor, guiding him toward their table.

"Have you ever been to a North Carolina beach?" Mike asked Maggie. She shook her head no. "I want to take you to a place where they play shag music. It's the only music you can dance to."

"Honestly, I have never heard of shag, but it sounds interesting," Maggie said, sitting him in the chair.

"You never heard of beach music?"

"I didn't know that it was a category, but it does sound fun. You ready for bed?" Maggie asked the next moment.

"Sure, let's go," Mike said, standing.

Maggie put her arm through his, leading him past the two men still standing against the bulkhead.

"Who were those meatheads?" Mike asked a little too loudly. He drew the attention of the other passengers around them—including Silas and Jay, who just smiled.

"Just guys from the neighborhood."

"'The neighborhood'"—his words slurred a bit—"as if you live in a *neighborhood*. You live in a country club, a gated community, the safest place in the whole world."

"They are associates of Alexandra."

"Aw, so they're from the *neighborhood*."

"What do you mean by that?" Maggie narrowed her eyes, waiting to defend her friend.

"I was the lead investigator on the Marco murder, if you don't remember."

"I won't ever forget. By the way, there was a murder behind those gates."

"I know all about Ms. Alex's associations—and her history. Just saying."

"We need to sit down."

Maggie led him to a chair near the door.

Mike sat leaning to the side. Maggie tried to hold him up. Kimberly and David saw her dilemma and came over.

"He's okay," Kimberly asked.

"I'm fine!" Mike said loud and defensively.

"How is Joanie holding up?" David asked to distract Mike.

"Surprisingly well," Maggie said.

"It helps that she didn't do anything wrong," Mike added, now hanging his head.

"I'm sorry, Mike, but we had to tell the truth," Kimberly said.

"I'm not blaming you, but you didn't see anything. You assumed what happened. There is no real evidence, and we need to find the body."

"I'm sure she did it, Mike," Kimberly said, looking at

David, who nodded his head in agreement. "If you had heard her voice… She was super pissed."

"Joanie swears John jumped from the balcony," Maggie said.

"Why would he jump?" David asked.

"That's what we need to find out," Mike said, slurring his words. "I think we should all get together tomorrow and figure it out." Mike was fading. "She didn't push him over, you know."

"I know we have a lot to figure out," Maggie said, patting his hand.

"Who is Silas?" he asked.

"We had a long day, sleep might clear all our heads," Maggie said, noticing how quickly Mike was fading.

David tilted his head toward Mike. "Do you need help?" he asked.

Maggie considered for a moment and then decided: "Yeah, I think I do."

She stood and held her hand out to Mike. He rose from his chair, not resisting. David took the other side, and Kimberly followed close behind.

Mike took carefully measured steps, letting Maggie and David lead him to the elevator and then straight to their suite.

Kimberly opened the door as Mike leaned against the wall. David and Maggie kept his body upright until they got him to his bed. He fell flat on his back. Before they could pull off his shoes and socks, he began to snore.

David laughed. "Sleep well."

"Thanks for the help," Maggie said, struggling to remove Mike's jacket and shirt. Unsure whether to remove his pants, she settled on taking off his belt and loosening the top button.

"Can you get me some headache powder?" Mike said, lying prone, his eyes shut tightly; but before Maggie could tell him she had no clue what "headache powder" was he was snoring again.

Maggie slipped into a pair of workout shorts and a T-shirt and got into bed, locating Mike's earbuds before settling in for the night. She pulled the covers up to her chin as she had as a child. She closed her eyes, feeling a little lost but a lot confused. Even with the earbuds, she could hear the rhythmic pattern of Mike snoring only a few feet away.

*

Maggie woke up as the sun made its way into the room. It felt like the ship was moving again. Hopefully they had found John's body—or better yet, perhaps they had found him alive. Maggie pulled the covers as she turned then realized she wasn't alone. A giant arm had flopped around her middle. She turned her head and faced Mike, who had climbed in next to her sometime during the night.

The alcohol must have done a number on her, too, because she had never felt him climb in. Maybe it was just wishful thinking, and she was still asleep. *Nope.* He was lying next to her, and she was confused about what to do about it. She wanted to snuggle up in his arms, but she didn't want to hope it was something that it was not.

Finally, Mike stirred. He was smiling.

"Good morning," he said.

"Good morning." Maggie smiled back. "You okay?"

"I'm good. Are *you* okay?" Mike asked with more of a concerned look on his face.

"Why wouldn't I be okay?" she asked.

"You were pretty upset last night, crying and yelling. I didn't know what to do."

Maggie panicked. "I *what*?"

"I think you had a bad dream. I didn't know if I should wake you up, so I just crawled in and put my arms around you, and you settled down."

"Wow, I don't remember any of that."

Mike kissed her on the top of her head then rolled over and sat up, stretching his back. Maggie watched him as he stood in only his underwear.

She turned over and shut her eyes tight, trying to burn the memory of his body into her brain and, at the same time, trying to remember what she could have been dreaming.

She opened her eyes only when she heard the shower start.

Maggie finally sat up to clear her head. She reached for the bottle of water Ralph staged on the nightstand every night. She drank it down, trying to quench the thirst she felt as well as ease her dry throat. It had been years since the night terrors—or at least years since someone other than her had witnessed them. Several times she had tried to record herself, but her utterings never made sense. She had gone to psychiatrists; they also had no explanation. It was embarrassing, but she usually just explained her terrors as a bad dream.

"What's headache powder?" Maggie asked Mike when he came out of the bathroom.

"You've never heard of headache powder?"

"No, and I've never heard of shagging, unless you were talking about, you know."

Mike laughed. "I *will* have to take you to the beach to shag."

"You said that last night, but I still don't know what you're talking about."

"It's a type of dancing, Maggie."

"Being in the South is like being in a foreign country," she said.

"Technically, we aren't in the South right now, and we are in a foreign country."

"Well, you got me there, big fella."

She smiled.

FRIDAY

CHAPTER 20

Bingo

"Bingo starts in fifteen minutes, anyone interested?" Maggie asked the group.

"I'm in."

David stood from where he had sat idly on the sofa next to Kimberly, who didn't bother to look up or acknowledge the question. She just turned the page of the novel she was reading. She was halfway through. Maggie looked over at Mike, who was sitting at the small table in the kitchen, examining some documents. He waved a rude dismissal, hitting Maggie in the gut.

"Let's go," she motioned to David, who followed her out the door. "I was under the impression that you weren't much of a gambler," she said once they had left the suite.

"Bingo isn't exactly gambling," David said. "It's still a game of chance, but someone in the room is going to win eventually. The only skill required is paying attention. No thinking involved."

"Honestly, David, you're such a smart guy, I'm surprised you don't play blackjack or something like that."

David laughed. "Funny you say that. I put myself through college playing poker."

"Poker?"

"And occasionally blackjack." He smiled. "But I was banned from casinos because they believed I was counting cards."

"Were you?" Maggie asked.

The elevator opened. David extended his arm, allowing Maggie to enter. They stood silently facing forward as the elevator sank until it reached Deck 5. David and Maggie exited into a small crowd that had already gathered and was making their way into the theater. When they made it to the front of the line a young man said, "It's five dollars each or five cards for twenty dollars."

"I'll take five cards," Maggie said. She fished a twenty dollar bill from her front pocket and handed it to the young man, who gave her five long cards and a pink dauber.

"What's this?" Maggie asked.

"It's how you mark your card. It's like a giant highlighter," the man said, looking behind Maggie at the line.

"I'll take five also," David said, trading his twenty dollar bill for five cards and a green dauber.

"You just wasted your money, I'm afraid," Maggie said, smiling. "The winning ticket is right here." She held up her cards.

"We shall see." David smiled and raised one eyebrow.

They took a seat midway up the center section, where there was a convenient ledge to place the drinks they had requested as soon as they were seated.

Maggie took a long sip of her Cabernet and took a deep breath. Relaxing for a few minutes felt good. The bingo was more popular with the passengers than the staff had anticipated, so processing everyone through the line took longer than expected. The delay provided Maggie the opportunity to find out a little more about David.

"Where did you go to school?" she asked.

"University of California, Riverside," David said.

"A west coast boy," Maggie said. "That doesn't surprise me."

"I grew up in Indio, California. My parents still live there today."

"So what on earth took you to Salisbury, North Carolina?"

"I had a friend in college from Charlotte, and when I was

looking for a job, my search included a fifty-mile radius. I honestly had no idea what I was getting into, but I ended up liking it."

"It's so far from your family."

"My family prefers it, I'm afraid. I wasn't such a good boy in my youth. My mother said I was too smart for my own good. School was boring, and I couldn't keep myself out of trouble."

"What kind of trouble?" Maggie asked.

"Mostly hacking. I was the first student to be expelled for breaking into the school's database and changing grades. Real amateur stuff, and I was caught pretty easy."

"How old were you?"

"Ten."

"That's pretty young to be hacking. You must have been smart."

"It always seems crazy to punish kids that young for using their brain. Maybe the schools should recognize the genius and refocus the kid in a different direction. The punishment could be staying after school so they can figure out how to make the system un-hackable. I don't know if that would have worked, but kicking me out of school just gave me more time to get in trouble."

"It seems like a big deal, but not that *big* of a deal, if you ask me."

"Nah, the real problem happened in junior high. I had this gym teacher, a real A hole. He loved to torture the kids who weren't athletically inclined, if you know what I mean." He drank the last of his mojito and signaled the server to bring two more, noticing Maggie's wine was almost gone.

"Okay, so what did you do?" Maggie sat at attention, figuring the conversation was going to get interesting.

"It's pretty bad, looking back at it now, but I might have set him up as a child molester. He made it to the sex offender register. It was bad."

"No, you didn't!"

"I did. The coach was arrested, fired, and almost divorced.

I basically ruined his life. Even when he was exonerated, some people assumed his guilt even when he was proved innocent. I think it's easier for people to believe bad things about people rather than see the good in them."

"That's horrible."

"I didn't think so at the time, because I was looking for revenge, but now looking at it from an adult perspective, I feel bad, even though he was a real jerk."

"How did you get caught?"

"My big mouth. I couldn't stand not getting the credit for such a feat. I had to hack into the police database, his personal computer, and the FBI's child pornography Special Agent system. It took coordination, and no one would have ever known, but I shared it with some of my gaming buddies, one of whom just happened to be one of those undercover cops trying to catch real child molesters. The next thing you know, an FBI task force storms our house, confiscates all the electronics and takes me to kiddy jail. Let me tell you, that is no place for a geek."

"Wow, David. That's horrible."

"I was a stupid kid using my brain to get back at that sadistic prick of a gym teacher."

"But you almost ruined his life!"

"I know, but I was only fourteen, so they weren't too hard on me. The worse part was that the cops were sure I had an accomplice. The prosecuting attorney put my poor parents through the wringer. They even had to take an extra mortgage on their house to cover the attorney fees."

"Yikes!"

"My parents emigrated from Mexico as children, and both worked hard. My mother still works in housekeeping at a resort in Palm Springs, and my father owns a very modest landscaping business. They didn't have the money to put me in boarding school, so they put me somewhere much worse."

"Juvie?"

"Ha! Worse. They made me live with my abuela."

"Abuela?"

"My grandmother on my father's side. She raised six boys and was proud that no one ever spent a night in jail. Her small home, located in a very rural area of Riverside County, was electronics free. The nearest neighbor was too far for me to tap into their internet. Her telephone was the kind with a dial. Have you ever seen one of those?"

"Unfortunately, I have. I even remember party lines."

"Huh?"

"Never mind," Maggie said, "please continue."

"My abuela was a taskmaster. 'Idle hands are the devil's workshop,' she would say, or something like that. You didn't talk back or question her authority in any way. She might have been under five feet tall, but she could wield a broom like Bruce Lee, and her aim with a slipper was sharper than Nolan Ryan's."

He pointed to his head. Maggie nodded in understanding.

Below them, Jules took the stage. "Welcome all to B-I-N-G-O, Bingo!" Jules wore her standard white uniform. Her hair was pulled into a close bun at the back of her head. "Are you ready for your first letter-number combination?"

The crowd yelled loudly and applauded.

Jules pulled a lever on the bingo cage that delivered a ball into a chamber. She pulled the ball out and announced, "B-4." She stood at the edge of the stage with a microphone in one hand and the small white ball in the other, holding it up as if the audience could see it from that far away. An electronic screen behind her lit up with the same square she announced: *B-4.*

Maggie and David punched their cards in the upper left corner. David looked down on his phone and hit a few numbers then put it into his pocket. Jules continued to call a few more letter-number combinations; G-59, O-74, B-13, I-21, B-10, O-70, B-2.

"I just need one more." David showed Maggie a card that was missing just N34.

Maggie looked down at her cards and took another drink of wine. "I'm not even close.

Jules continued calling out the combinations: "G-55,

N-42, I-20, N-34."

"BINGO!" David yelled. He stood straight up, almost knocking over his drink, which was sitting on the ledge in front of him.

"We have a possible winner," Jules announced. "Everyone sit tight while we validate the card."

The young man who had been distributing the cards earlier climbed the stairs that led to the railing in front of where David and Maggie were sitting. A second young man stood alongside him. David handed over his lucky card. One of the young men read off the punches while the other typed into an iPad. The man holding the card held it up and announced, "We have a winner!" He then doled out five $100 bills into David's eager hand.

"Congratulations!" Jules pronounced from the stage. "Don't be disappointed, everyone, we will continue to play the cards you have—but to win, you must have all the squares that make an *X* across your card."

David sat back down, folding the bills in half and placing them in his front jeans pocket.

"Great job," Maggie said. Five hundred bucks. You're rich."

David smiled and took a drink from his glass. "Thanks."

"You're a lucky guy," Maggie said.

"Am I?" David laughed and took out his phone. Maggie saw what looked like a picture of his BINGO card on his phone screen.

"No way you manipulated that," she said quietly, looking around. "I thought you said it was a game of chance."

"It *used* to be a game of chance when the balls were simply ping pong balls in a cage that you cranked by hands, but each of those balls is individually electronically marked, so when one of the balls is placed in the tray, it registers up there on the screen and the caller reads it off their I-pad. It was an easy algorithm to break. I just hijacked the signal of the balls on my card and I say Bingo!"

"So, you just cheated at BINGO?" Maggie asked in a low

voice, barely louder than a whisper.

"It's called using tools to your advantage, not cheating," he said, not even showing an ounce of guilt. "No harm, no foul."

"I'm surprised you don't play the lottery," Maggie said.

"Too much attention." He smiled. "There are way easier ways to make money."

That's interesting, Maggie, thought, but decided to drop it. David's skills were impressive. She decided not to focus on how he could have pulled the whole thing off...or was he just lucky.

"Have you ever played BINGO before?"

"Ha!" He smiled. "I have but not to win very much. The secret is always to stay invisible. People don't notice small takes from quiet people."

Did he just admit that he is a thief? It was the first time Maggie considered David as a real suspect. But would he take money from an old lady?

"How do you think Kimberly won at the slot tournament the other day?"

"There is no way you were able to hack into a casino's slots. Their security is better than Fort Knox."

"That's true *most of the time*, but when they set up a slot tournament, they bypass the main security, and they let the wheels just go. It doesn't need to track winnings by machine, but each machine does have a code that I tapped into."

"I can't believe you helped her win," Maggie said.

"I'm not going to help her win the finals. I thought she just needed something to be happy about, and I think it worked. She's been in a great mood."

"I don't know, David; cheating is cheating."

"Who did it hurt? It was just a stupid game. All chance. It doesn't matter to anyone."

Maggie fell silent. It wasn't her job to judge other people; but what David had done was manipulative, even to Kimberly, who thought she had won fair and square.

"I just think you could use your talents for good," Maggie said.

"Exactly." David agreed, but Maggie realized that David's *good* and her *good* were very different goods. If he was willing to manipulate a slot machine for Kimberly, what else would he do? Of all the people who could bypass the red flags at the bank, David seemed the most likely candidate.

"You seem way too smart to be working in a small-town bank in the middle of North Carolina. It makes me wonder why you aren't working for law enforcement or some high tech company?" Maggie tried not to sound like she was interrogating him.

"Money isn't everything, Maggie." He turned to her and looked straight into her eyes. "There are more important things in life."

"BINGO!" someone yelled from the balcony above them.

The numbers were quickly verified, and the winner was paid her cash.

"I guess that's it," Maggie said, standing and stretching her back and neck. She wanted to talk to David some more, but with the crowd quickly filtering out of the auditorium and Jules wrapping things up onstage, the opportunity had passed.

CHAPTER 21

Art Auction

"Can I ask you a question?" Maggie said as she followed David out of the auditorium and through the main corridor.

"Sure, ask away," he said, not turning around. Maggie hurried to his side.

"Do you like Kimberly?"

"Yeah, she is very likable."

"No"—Maggie shook her head,—"do you *like* like her?"

David smiled as he continued to walk. "Are you asking me if we are having some illicit affair, or am I falling for her flirty help-the -damsel-in-distress routine?"

"I guess I'm asking both?"

They passed a bar called the Dolphin, where David stopped. Every seat was occupied. All the patrons were in the middle of a group trivia contest. He motioned Maggie to stand next to him then leaned on the divider at the bar, not answering her question but distracted by the announcer's questions.

"Billy Joel," David whispered to Maggie.

"Before the cruise," Maggie said, resuming her questioning, "did you and Kimberly hang out?"

David didn't answer Maggie. He was now focused on the next question. "What is the most popular single of all time?" the announcer asked.

David turned his head to Maggie. "That's an easy one, 'Candle in the Wind.'"

"Easy for you," she said. "You know a lot about music."

"It's my passion. You can ask me anything—rock and roll, techno, country, opera, you name it, I love it. Music makes sense. It's universal."

"Did you ever play in a band?"

"The Fyre Festival," he said to Maggie. She looked confused.

"The answer to the trivia question is the Fyre Festival." He said it a little too loudly, giving the group of passengers sitting at the closest table the answer. They smiled and wrote it down. Other people looked over at him suspiciously.

"We should go," Maggie said, pulling at David's arm.

He smiled. "Probably."

As they moved down the corridor, they observed some activity ahead.

"Hey." David pointed. "The art auction is going on, let's go." He reached out and grabbed Maggie's hand then led her into another crowed space.

"This ought to be fun."

"Oh, God, I can't."

Maggie pulled back as they drew closer to the crowd, which was packed in like sardines.

"Oh yeah, I forgot." David smiled and looked around. He pointed to the bulkhead. "Stand here for a second." Maggie moved back a few steps and leaned against the cold surface. She watched the people walk by until David reappeared a few minutes later.

He motioned to her and called, "Follow me."

He pulled her to the right of the crowd, where there was a clear path around the group. They made their way behind several tables with large flat boxes on top. They walked a bit farther until they were standing directly behind two six-foot-long tables covered by black tablecloths. A server dressed in a tux shirt and black vest poured champagne into flutes lined up at the front of the table. The server looked confused seeing Maggie standing behind the long table, but if he was bothered by it at all, he didn't let it show. He just smiled and continued to pour champagne into the glasses.

Several similarly dressed servers roved through the crowd carrying trays of appetizers. David stood between the two tables, and as one of the servers passed him, he picked up a miniature quiche and a cucumber sandwich. He offered one to Maggie, but she simply shook her head.

Maggie relaxed, standing behind her barrier of tables and even helping herself to a glass of champagne. She watched small paddles stamped with numbers rise above the crowd as the auctioneer acknowledged the bidders. The auctioneer didn't speak fast, as she had imagined, but was still a little hard to understand because of his accent.

"Would you like some?" A server coming from a back area held out a small pitcher of what looked like orange juice. "For a mimosa?" he asked.

"Yes, please." Maggie smiled, hearing Britney's voice in her head: *The only cure for cheap champagne is orange juice.*

She tasted the beverage. "Oh, this is good," she said to the man, now filling half of the glasses in front of her.

"It's mango orange," the server said, smiling. David picked up a glass of the sparkly orange drink and stood next to Maggie.

David held his drink toward the crowd. "What do you think?"

"I always wondered why people bought art on a cruise ship and how they get it home." Maggie said.

"There are novice collectors who look forward to this event; the cruise line ships it for free."

Maggie nodded. She pointed to a small painting of Van Gogh's *Starry Night* that was on display. It was the next painting to go on auction. "That's a cool one."

"Also one of my favorites," David said. He turned to Maggie. "Just stay here, I'll be right back." He set his drink on the table and disappeared into the crowd.

Okay, Maggie said to herself. She finished her drink, replacing the empty glass with a full one.

"This is a convenient place to stand."

Silas' hot breath hit Maggie's ear, causing the hairs on the back of her neck to rise.

Maggie turned to Silas "What are you doing here?".

"Just wrapping things up," Silas said.

"At an art auction?"

"Hopefully." He smiled a big toothy smile as he put his hand on Maggie's hip, causing her further discomfort.

"One hundred dollars, two hundred dollars, do I hear three hundred dollars?" The auction had started back up, but Maggie was distracted by Silas.

"Can you stick around for a few minutes after this is over?" Silas' face had turned sober. "I have a favor to ask,"

"I don't know, I—" Maggie turned when David tapped her on the shoulder.

"I got it," he said proudly, holding out an envelope out to Maggie.

"What's this?"

"*Starry Night*," he smiled. "For you."

Maggie opened the envelope. Inside was a certificate. "All you have to do is give them your address, and they'll ship it." He pointed to a woman sitting behind a desk.

The last shout of "*Sold!*" hung in the air as the quiet patrons in the crowd all began talking at the same time. Shortly afterwards, most of the passengers had moved along to other parts of the ship.

"Thank you for the picture, David, but it seems like these sorts of replicas are available almost anywhere. Why makes it so special to be in an auction?"

"It's an F-A, forgery art."

"What?" Maggie tilted her head in confusion.

"It's legal," David said, "it's a thing. Legal forgery. There are actual forgery artists who are more renowned than the artists who actually painted the originals. Somehow it created a whole new market in art. If you think about it, it's pure genius."

"So interesting...I'm excited to have my first real fake-not fake piece of art," Maggie said. "Thank You."

"You are welcome." He smiled. "I used my bingo winnings."

"You spent five hundred dollars on a painting that is an actual forgery?"

"It was four hundred and twenty dollars; it would have been less, but I was bidding against a stubborn old lady. I'm still up a couple of bucks." David looked at his watch. "I need to get back to the room, do you want me to wait for you?"

Maggie looked at the line of people at the sales desk.

"No, you go back to the room. I'll wait here until the line dies down." Maggie picked up another mimosa. "I'll be fine."

David smiled and started to walk away.

"Thanks again, David," Maggie said. "That was such a nice thing to do."

David again told her she was welcome. Then he said, "See you later." He left with a slight wave.

Maggie saw Silas now standing on the other side of the now almost empty room. She stood enjoying her drink as the line dwindled until there was only one person left in the queue before she stood in front of the desk.

When it was her turn, Maggie handed the woman the envelope David gave her.

"How is your day going?" the woman asked as she wrote down the information on the card into a journal on the desk.

"It's been a pretty good day so far," Maggie said.

"*Starry Night,*" the woman said as she handed the certificate back to Maggie. "I love this one."

"Me too," Maggie said.

"What address would you like the painting delivered to?"

Maggie started reciting her address at Banyan Tree Country Club. But a loud crash from behind her caused her to jump. The table where Maggie had stood earlier had flipped onto its side. What was left of the glass champagne flutes lay in a shattered mess on the floor.

Silas reached behind Maggie. He pulled the journal from the desk and whispered in Maggie's ear: "Meet me at the wine bar." Maggie turned fast enough to see Silas disappear around the corner.

She stood for a moment, confused. The woman, who had also been distracted by the commotion, turned her attention back to the desk. She fumbled through the stacks of paperwork, apparently looking for the journal where she had been recording addresses.

"Did you see that book I was writing in?" she asked Maggie.

Maggie shook her head. She avoided the woman's suspicions by focusing her eyes back on the mess behind her. Several people were picking up the shattered glass and using towels to soak up the spilled champagne.

The woman continued to riffle through the paperwork; she even pulled the chair out to search under it. Maggie took the opportunity to head to the wine bar. She made a quick stop at the bathroom to relieve the pressure that had built up from the two glasses of champagne and one orange mango.

As soon as she walked into the wine bar, she spotted Silas with a bucket of beer and a glass of red wine. He was sitting at the same table they had sat before. She slid in next to him and pointed to the glass. He pushed the glass to her, and she took a sip. Then she tilted her head at Silas. "Okay, let's hear it?".

Silas pulled the journal from the seat next to him and set it on the table.

"There are addresses on this list that are part of a drug conspiracy."

"That's the case you're working?" Maggie asked.

"We have it pretty much wrapped up now." He held up the pages and set them back next to him on the bench seat.

"What do art aficionados have to do with drugs?"

"The addresses in this book will tell us exactly where the art will be delivered"—he patted the journal—"with their frames filled with cocaine. Whoever accepts delivery of the package are the distributors. End of the line."

"You took the addresses, so how will they know who to

deliver to?”

“I’ll make copies and drop it off at lost and found.”

“Impressive, Silas. Now tell me, how did the drugs get on board in the first place?”

“The divemaster brings them on board. He swaps an empty oxygen tank for a tank filled with cocaine during the dive trip. He loads the tank with all the other dive tanks then fills the frames with the drugs. The dive equipment locker is in the same storage room as the frames. They assemble the art the night before the auction. Several people bid on any piece of art with a black frame and then give the addresses of the receivers.”

“How did you figure it all out?”

“Jay and I followed the divemaster on our dive excursion. We watched him swap the tanks at the bottom of the ocean. It’s extremely dangerous and difficult to do, but he swapped the tanks with hardly any effort. We also attached a tracker on his uniform and recorded him in that storage room for a long time. When we checked it out, we found the drugs.”

“What did you do with the drugs?”

“Nothing, we left them in the frames but attached a tracking device to each one so the D-E-A can locate and arrest the guys at the end of the line.”

“Does my painting have drugs in the frame?

“If it did, your friend would have lost the bid. It’s all set up.”

“So, you solved your case?”

“Not one hundred percent. We got the middle and the end figured out, but what we don’t have is the guys responsible for the air tank at the bottom of the ocean.”

“Isn’t that the most important guy?”

“Yep, that’s why we’ll head back to Cozumel. We had to figure out how it played out on board the ship. We have limited jurisdiction on the Mexican side, so it’s a little touchy. It’s likely the cartels, and they might be hard to infiltrate, but at least we interrupted another avenue for their delivery into the United States.”

"Well, be careful, it seems a little dangerous for two civilians to be taking on," Maggie said.

"Civilians? Maggie, you have no idea, but don't worry about us. You might want to focus on your boyfriend."

"What do you mean? And he is not my boyfriend."

"He checked us out with the security on board."

"What do you mean, checked you out?"

"He went to Randolph and said we were suspicious. Randolph played it off. He couldn't tell him we were on the job. Some detective you got there." He laughed. "I'm surprised you haven't filled him in on who we are."

"Obviously I don't know 'who you are,' and I just didn't want to expose too much, especially for Alex's sake. You saved my life once. I owe you that much. Plus, I don't know if Mike is covering for his sister. I just don't have anything figured out yet, so I decided to keep my cards close."

"Well, I'm impressed. You might make a good detective."

Silas smiled again, but Maggie ignored his attempts to be charming. Her brain was busy thinking about David and one of the things he had said about Kimberly. "*Her damsel-in-distress routine.*" What did he mean by that? Also, was Joanie using Mike to cover her tracks—and if he figured it out, was he going to keep silent?

SATURDAY

CHAPTER 22

Grand Cayman

"I honestly don't feel like going off the ship today," Maggie said.

"I was feeling the same way," Mike said. "Let's go have breakfast and then go talk to Joanie. I thought of a few things I wanted to ask her."

They made their way to Deck 5, where they turned toward the main dining room. Maggie froze. She whispered to Mike: "That's the guy we saw talking to John at breakfast the day I passed out. Remember the bartender?"

"How do you know?" he asked.

"It's him. I'm sure," Maggie said. "It looks like him from the back anyway."

"Except he's in civilian clothes, so how can you be sure?"

"I'm not one hundred percent sure, but it's a lead. Let's follow him. He's probably heading off the ship. He's carrying the backpack," Maggie said, pulling Mike in order to have him follow her.

"What the heck, we don't have anything better to do," Mike said.

They followed the man at a safe distance as he walked off the gangway and stepped onto the pier. He did look like John from the back, Maggie thought. The air was thick, and it was already hot. Maggie wished she had remembered to put on some sunblock as they walked several blocks, careful to keep enough distance from the man so as not to be detected.

They continued to follow him until he reached Cayman Island National Bank, where he disappeared through the automatic doors.

"Now what?" Maggie asked. "Should we follow him in?"

"Why not, he doesn't know who we are." Mike started for the door. When they walked in, they saw the man's back at a teller station. They stood at the center counter where the deposit and withdrawal slips were stacked. They watched as a bank employee dressed in a white linen suit came and led the man into a back office. As the man turned, both Maggie and Mike ducked. It wasn't the bartender they had been following. It was John. He was alive.

As soon as he disappeared into the office, Mike grabbed Maggie's arm and pulled her out of the doors of the bank. His face looked panicked.

"He's alive," Maggie said, "but he isn't…"

"Obviously," Mike said. "I can't believe my eyes. He's *alive*."

"What do we do now?" Maggie said.

"I'm going to try to take a picture with my phone," Mike said. "It will be proof that Joanie didn't push him overboard. She was telling the truth."

"Do you think he has the money in the backpack?"

"It was all issued in cashier's checks, but if he did convert it to cash, it's probably the reason why he drove to Fort Lauderdale instead of flying with the rest of us. He couldn't transport that much cash on a plane. You have to declare anything over ten grand."

"How did he get it on the ship?"

"Security isn't as careful on a ship. They're looking for someone to sneak on a bottle of wine or a bit of marijuana."

"Surely not a million bucks and a couple of pounds of cocaine?"

Mike looked at Maggie with narrow eyes. "What?"
"Never mind."
Mike motioned for Maggie to follow him behind a small

silver thatch palm clump at the corner of the building.

It was almost a half hour before John came out of the bank. He still had the backpack slung over his shoulder; it appeared to be quite a bit flatter. Whatever he had in there, he might have left in the bank, Maggie thought.

John paused at the top step of the bank and looked around. Mike and Maggie remained hidden until John reached the bottom of the steps. Instead of walking back the way he came, he headed north toward the place where they were hiding. Mike leaned over Maggie and snapped a few pictures.

"Hopefully, I got a good enough picture to get Joanie released."

"But what about the money?" Maggie asked.

"Well, at least we know where it is, if that's what he was doing at the bank." Mike snapped a few more pictures, but now he could only get John's backside.

"What else would he be doing in a Cayman Island bank?"

"And why would he fake his death?" Mike asked.

"I know someone who could find out," Maggie said as they watched John disappear around the corner of the bank. He was going in the opposite direction of the ship.

"He's not going back," Mike said.

"Let's keep following him and see where he goes," Maggie suggested. Mike had already started back toward the bank. When they reached the corner, they paused before exposing themselves. John just continued walking down the block toward the center of the island.

"He sure looks like he knows where he's going," Mike said.

They cautiously walked two blocks behind John, sticking to the side of the street closer to the buildings in case they had to duck in somewhere. But it wasn't far enough. John stopped in the middle of the sidewalk, adjusted his backpack, and turned abruptly down a side alley.

They were not sure if that was his route or if he had even spotted them. Maggie and Mike ran until they came to the edge of the block. Mike held Maggie back with one arm as he took a step around the building. He yelped. Maggie rushed to Mike who was now laying on the ground holding his head. John had obviously been waiting in the alley with a stray brick that was now laying on the ground next to where Maggie knelt.

"Are you okay?" she asked.

It took Mike a moment to respond. "I can't believe that just happened." He tried to sit up but lay back on the cement.

"Should I get help?" Maggie asked. She looked up but did not see anyone—especially not John.

"I'm okay," he said, keeping his eyes closed. "Give me a second."

Maggie sat helplessly, looking around for anyone who might be able to help, but no one came, and she didn't want to leave Mike alone. The next five minutes seemed like five hours, but finally Mike sat up, rubbing his head. Maggie stood and offered her hand. Mike took it but used his other hand to leverage himself to his feet.

"You okay?" Maggie asked again.

"I actually saw stars," Mike said, shaking his head and a little unsteady on his feet.

"I think he hit you with this brick." Maggie held up a red clay block lying next to the spot where Mike had fallen. "Maybe we'll have matching bumps," she said, throwing the brick away..

"I totally underestimated that guy," Mike admitted as he held on to the side of the building. He wanted to make sure he was steady on his feet before actually taking a step. He looked around as if he expected to see John, but he was gone. "I guess we should just head back to the ship,. Mike's face was full of disappointment.

"At least we got proof that Joanie didn't kill him."

Mike pulled his phone from his pocket and looked at the screen.

"What I don't understand is how he got off the boat without some kind of alarm going off," Maggie said. "You have to show your sail card." She held up the card that hung at the end of the lanyard. "How did he fake being pushed off the boat?"

"John is an adrenaline junkie. I didn't think about it at the time but we went bungee jumping in Honduras.

"Bungie jumping?"

"Yes, you know, we did that as part of our shore excursion," he said.

"Do you think he bungee jumped off the balcony?"

"No, someone would have seen him, and where would he get the elastic rope on board the ship?" Mike asked. "But remember the list of rock climbing equipment? He likes extreme sports, and there's a rock climbing wall over by the volleyball courts on Deck 10. Maybe he figured out how to configure some of the equipment."

"Maybe. Do you think the bartender helped him get the equipment?" Maggie asked.

"Not only that, I think he used his identity. We'll find out soon enough."

Maggie saw a taxi cab and waved her arm. The car pulled over, and she helped Mike climb into the taxi. He still was not quite steady on his feet. As soon as the taxi began heading back to the pier, she breathed in deep.

"I actually saw stars," Mike said again.

"I think you need to be checked out by the doctor on board. I'm afraid you might have a concussion."

"I'll be fine." Mike tried to smile but winced. "So, you started to say earlier something about someone who could help us find out something...."

"David," Maggie said excitedly. "Now that we know John took the money, we can ask David to help us recover it. He's a genius."

"Do you think he could break into a Cayman Island bank's system?" Mike asked.

"I don't know, but he is pretty smart, and he does work at a bank. I think we should at least ask him."

Mike leaned his head gently back against the car seat. "What if he's an accomplice?"

"I think we need to take a chance that he isn't."

The taxi pulled up to the entrance to the pier. Maggie pulled out a U.S. twenty dollar bill and handed it to the driver. "Keep the change," she said, looking at the blood the injury on Mike's head had left on the seat, "And—sorry."

"No problem."

The driver reached down to the passenger side of his taxi and tore off a wad of paper towels from a roll he kept there.

"Thanks." Maggie handed Mike the wad of paper towels. She kept her arm through his to keep him steady as they made their way over to the gangway.

As soon as they reached the ship, Maggie placed her handbag on the conveyer belt for inspection. Mike walked through the checkpoint but stood at a small table where a ship's security guard also stood by to examine suspicious bags.

"Can you locate Randolph Edwards for me?" Mike asked.

"What do you need with the head of security?" the guard asked suspiciously.

"Just tell him it's Mike Marker, and I have some information he might be interested in."

The man picked up his walkie talkie, and after some back and forth, he told Mike: " "He'll meet you in the purser's office in fifteen minutes. Do you know where that is?"

"Yes, thanks," Mike said. He headed for the elevators with Maggie in tow.

When they reached Deck 4, Randolph was waiting for them.

"Wow, what happened to you?" Randolph asked. "Do you need a doctor?"

"Never mind my head," Mike said. "Take a look at this."

Mike pulled out his phone and scrolled to the pictures he had taken in town. He held his phone to Randolph.

"Who is that?" Randolph asked.

"That's John," Mike said impatiently.

"Well, I'll be." Randolph said, "He's alive."

"Not only is he alive, but he was also hiding somewhere on this ship," Maggie said. "We followed him this morning."

"Impossible," Randolph said.

"Obviously not impossible," Maggie returned. "We also think he may have used climbing equipment from the rock wall to stage his fall overboard."

"Well, that's easy to figure out," Randolph said. He unfastened his walkie talkie from his belt then spoke directly into it: "Can you meet me on Deck 11?"

A disembodied voice answered: *"Roger that."*

Looking at Mike, Randolph added, "Can you also stop by the infirmary and bring an ice pack?"

"You got it, chief."

After ending the communications with his assistant, Randolph turned back to Mike and Maggie. "Let's go up to the balcony in your suite." He reached and pushed the *Up* button behind them.

When they reached the door to the suite, Randolph used his master key card to let them in. He walked straight to the sliders, ignoring David and Kimberly, who were sitting next to each other on the couch. Randolph pulled out his key ring and thumbed through the keys until he located the one he wanted; then he removed the lock and slid out the chain, allowing access to the balcony. Mike and Maggie followed him behind the hot tub. He leaned over the rail, careful not to touch it. "Well, you could be onto something." He turned to face them. "There are definitely some gouges in the paint that could have been made by rigging gear."

His walkie talkie squealed to life. He walked away from Mike and Maggie and spoke more instructions. His assistant showed up and joined them on the balcony. He handed the ice pack to Mike, who was obviously in need.

Randolph once again joined them. "They're missing several pieces of gear from the rock wall."

"So, I guess you can release my sister?"

"I would rather not, but I will if you promise to keep her quiet and make sure she doesn't leave this suite. She's an eyewitness, and when we pull into port tomorrow, I need her to be available."

"Done," Mike said.

"Is there anything else I can do for you?"

"I'll let you know. Thanks." Mike shook Randolph's hand. "Just get my sister released."

"You got it."

"There's one more thing," Mike said, "do you think we could get access to the ship's computer?"

Plenty of computers are available in the business center," Randolph said.

"They have too many filters and protections. We need one that can bypass the security features set up by the ship."

"I think I can have our I-T department set something up for you in this room."

"That would be great," Mike said.

"Whatever you find, I need to be the first to know." Randolph looked back and forth between Mike and Maggie. "Okay?"

"Definitely," Mike said.

Randolph ushered them back through the sliding glass doors before he threaded the chain back through the handles and locked it, pulling on the lock to ensure it fastened.

"I'll send up the I-T crew as soon as possible," Randolph said.

David perked up. "I-T crew?" He looked at Mike.

"They are going to set up a computer free of the security restrictions—and we're going to need your help," Mike said.

"I'm in," David said, smiling, not even having a clue what he had agreed to do.

When the equipment showed up, David barely let the IT crew get it in the door when he took over. He set the monitor on the bar between the kitchen and living area. He requested a few things, which the IT staff quickly brought up.

Maggie watched in fascination as it all came to life. David had requested an additional monitor so he could look at multiple screens at the same time. Mike stood behind David, giving him the name and address of the bank John had walked into earlier that morning.

David's fingers flew over the keys, but he shook his head. "It's not like our bank. They have a firewall I can't get past."

"You can get past the firewall at your bank?" Maggie asked.

"Well, yes," he said proudly, "that's my job, to make sure others can't."

Or if you wanted to take money out of someone's account and set someone else up for it, you could, Maggie thought.

Mike saw the concern on Maggie's face and came over to where she was standing. "You okay?" he said.

Maggie turned and took a step away from where David was engrossed in his task.

"Are we sure David didn't have anything to do with this?" she whispered. "Maybe he helped John?"

"Do we have any other option at this point?"

"I guess not," she said.

David looked up from the keyboard. "Do you have any account numbers from the bank?"

"Um, no," Mike said.

"Why do you need one?" Maggie asked.

"In order to get past the firewall I have to enter a string of numbers into an alphanumeric field. It looks the numbers might be embedded in an account number. If I could get one account number, I could work through it. If I had two, I could break it even faster."

"How can we get an account number?" Mike asked to no one in particular.

"I have an idea," Maggie said.

Maggie pulled her phone from her backpack. "I know someone who could help," she said, scrolling through her contacts until she came to Alexandra's name. Several contact numbers were listed. Maggie started with Alex's cell phone, which went directly to voicemail, so she hung up, not bothering to leave a message that she knew would go unanswered. Alex was modern in many ways, but not when it came to technology.

Maggie then chose Alex's work number. Alex answered on the second ring.

Maggie explained the story to Alex and then stayed silent, holding the phone to her ear for a long while. Finally, she motioned for the pen and pad of paper sitting next to the phone. She jotted down a few numbers and letters and repeated what she wrote.

"That's it," David said aloud, "they use letters." He continued to tap the keys and finally sat back, stretching his arms behind him.

"Did you get it?" Mike asked.

"It's running now."

"I'll get a list of all deposits made today, but it's going to take a bit of time."

Chef Paul entered the suite at that moment. They all turned and looked at him.

"Did I interrupt something?" he said, looking around.

"Nope. You're right on time if you're here to make lunch," David said.

"I would be happy to," Chef Paul said. He smiled and headed for the kitchen. Just then, the door clicked again, and Ralph stepped in, holding it open. Joanie walked in.

Joanie ran to Mike and threw her arms around him. "I am *so* sorry for how I treated you," she said.

Mike wrapped his arms around her. "I understand. This whole thing has been hard on everyone, especially you."

Maggie watched the interaction, understanding how Joanie and Mike's warm embrace in the aftermath of their argument with one another must be typical of their relationship.

Ralph came back from the kitchen and approached Mike. "Randolph Edwards would like to speak with you, if you have some time. He has some vital information for you."

Mike looked over at David, who still was leaning back in his chair, arms across his chest. "It will be a while," he said to Mike, sensing Mike's reluctance to leave.

Mike waved to Maggie to join him.

As soon as they entered the purser's office, Maggie gasp. Sitting with his back towards them was John...but when he turned around, Maggie realized it wasn't John but the bartender. Maggie again was stunned by how much the bartender resembled John: similar height and weight—and, of course, an identical bald head. But when he had turned, the similarity ended. The man had a broad nose with a white scar across it.

"This is Vlado Kovacs," Randolph said. The man stood and turned toward Mike and Maggie. He nodded his head in greeting. Mike returned the gesture. "It seems your associate, Mr. Haas, had made arrangements with Mr. Kovacs to use his I-D."

"He made it impossible to deny his request," the man said in a heavy accent.

"What do you mean?" Maggie asked.

"He showed me a badge and said it was official business."

"It seems Mr. Haas was posing as a government official and convinced Mr. Kovacs to participate," Randolph said.

"I didn't know," the bartender said again.

"You can go for now," Randolph told the man.

Maggie moved aside to let the bartender pass. As soon as he left the room, Randolph held up some ropes and carabiners attached to what looked like a harness of some kind. "We also found this stashed in one of the lifeboats. It seems that's where John was hiding."

"In a lifeboat?" Mike asked.

"Yes, there was bedding, a food stash, and, unfortunately, what appears to be several bottles of urine."

"Gross," Maggie said.

"He was a Special Forces marine. I just don't understand why he took such measures."

"I radioed ahead to the Coast Guard and the local authorities in Broward County. Have you two figured out why he would fake his own death to escape to the Cayman Islands?"

"We haven't figured that out yet," Mike said, "but we'll let you know as soon as we find something."

"All right. We're leaving this port soon and will arrive in

Fort Lauderdale by morning. I'm meeting with the locals before we leave here."

*

As soon as they returned to the suite, Mike and Maggie saw Kimberly and David sitting at the computer, their faces drawn close to the monitors.

"I got a list of accounts," David said without turning around, "but I didn't see John's name on any accounts at this bank. Are you sure he isn't using an alias?"

"How about Vlado Kovacs?" Mike said, moving to the computer. David and Kimberly moved aside to let him get a closer look. Mike took his reading glasses out of his front pocket, settling them near the end of his nose. He put his finger on the mouse and rolled it around for a while. Suddenly his face changed.

"What?" Maggie said.

He looked at the three of them. "Nothing."

Just then Joanie came out of her room. She had wrapped a towel around her head. "Did you find something?" she asked.

Mike pushed the power button causing the monitor to go blank.

"Why did you do that?" Maggie asked looking at David who shook his head.

"It was a dead end," Mike said.

"He was at the bank," Maggie said. "We saw him there."

"But we didn't see him *actually* deposit any money. We only saw him enter an office, and he still had the backpack when we followed him. He could simply have rented a safety deposit box." Mike started to pull the wires from the computer.

Ralph came into the room. "Does anyone need a drink?"

"Please," Mike said. "Amaretto sour."

"I'll take a Cabernet," Maggie said.

"Margarita," Joanie said.

"Make that two," Kimberly said.

"Three," David indicated.

"You got it." Ralph moved to the other side of the bar. He

fixed Maggie's drink first: all it involved was pouring the wine from the opened bottle. Maggie took the filled glass from the counter and sat at the far side of the room, looking out the large glass windows.

"Why don't we go sit on the small balcony in our room?" Mike held out a hand to Maggie. She took Mike's hand and followed him through their room to the balcony. Mike pulled out one of the two plastic chairs and allowed Maggie to sit.

"I thought we had him," Maggie said, confused by the look on Mike's face.

"That's the thing, Maggie. I did see something."

"What?"

"There was an account that received nine hundred thousand dollars this morning."

"And?" She tilted her head.

"The name on the account was Mildred Brown."

"Your Aunt Millie?"

"The one and only."

"Is it a setup?"

"Possibly, but I honestly don't think so." Mike hung his head.

"You're saying Aunt Millie, a ninety-three-year-old woman, is somehow connected to John Haas in a scheme to defraud your sister's bank?"

"It seems ridiculous," Mike said, "but that is what it appears to be. Technically, though, it's her own money, so I don't think it would be defrauding anything."

"I can't get my head around this," Maggie said. "Your aunt, that sweet old lady?"

"I've known this woman my whole life"—Mike tilted his head—"but, honestly, in the very back of my brain, I just might believe it, even if I don't want to."

Maggie looked confused. "But why would she do it?"

"That's what we are going to find out."

SUNDAY

CHAPTER 23

Disembarkation

Getting off the ship was always so much worse than getting on. The suitcases had to be packed and sitting outside the room the night before. Clothes and essentials for the next day had to fit in a carry-on.

Maggie's suitcase was full of dirty, messy clothes, a good representation of her current state of mind. She had a fitful night, waking up several times, thinking it was already time to get up.

Finally, morning came. The group said their goodbyes to Chef Paul as he handed them each a small brown bag with an egg sandwich, fruit, and a pastry. Then they walked out the door of the suite. Maggie was the last to leave. She stopped one last time to look back at the room they had just spent the previous week in. It had all happened so fast.

Ralph herded them down to the VIP lounge, where he left them to wait for their disembarkation instructions. Joanie handed him an envelope as he said his final goodbyes. Then he hurried back to get the OASIS suite ready for the next group.

Joanie sat on one side of a small table, facing Mike and Maggie. She looked refreshed and was smiling. It was as if she had never spent a night behind bars.

"Have you two figured out how we're going to get Aunt Millie's money back?" Joanie asked.

"That's the thing, Joanie," Mike said. "The money might not be missing."

"Of course it's missing," Joanie said a little too loudly, causing passengers sitting nearby to turn.

Mike leaned in, keeping his voice low. "It was Aunt Millie's money, and Aunt Millie's name is on the account."

Joanie didn't flinch but tightened her lips.

"Did you know anything about this?" Maggie asked but instantly regretted getting in the middle of the siblings. Joanie's eyes filled with ice.

"If you..."

She stopped, and the ice melted. "Of course I didn't know anything about this," she said in a sugary tone but kept her back teeth closed.

Mike's knee pushed against Maggie's thigh. Maggie leaned back and smiled, leaving any unspoken words to roam around in her head.

Joanie looked down at her phone. She became distracted by whatever she was looking at while the other two remained silent until their turn came to disembark the ship.

The line to get through customs was long even though their VIP status allowed them to be among the first to disembark. The group formed a human shield around Maggie; Mike took the left and Joanie the right, Kimberly the front, and David the back. They now took warnings of Maggie's panic attacks seriously. Maggie focused on her steps, not looking around.

It seemed like the longest week of her life. Even having access to all the amenities of the luxury suite, she needed space. She was homesick for her home in Boca Raton, her friends gathering at the bar for happy hour and arguing over the stupidest club rules. Even the thick Florida air was a welcoming hug. She wished she could just stay in Boca. Her home was only thirty minutes away, but her car was in North Carolina.

She had planned to head to the mountains before her trip back to Boca, but maybe she would just drive down the west coast of Florida to decompress.

"How are you doing?" Mike asked, noticing Maggie's faraway look.

"I'm good, just focusing on anything other than all these people. I can't believe how many people they put on these ships —and to think in a few more hours just as many will be boarding." Maggie took a deep breath and let it out slowly. Then, not too much longer, they were through the line and out the door to the terminal where their driver stood waiting on them. He took Maggie's bag and helped her up the single step into the black Sprinter van, where she stepped to the back seat. Mike was right behind her and took the spot next to her. Joanie climbed into the front passenger seat.

"What's next?" she asked as soon as the van was moving.

"As soon as we get home, I'm going to visit my aunt."

"Not without me," Joanie observed from the seat in front of Mike.

"Of course," Mike said. "You and Maggie are coming with me."

"I can't go," Maggie said quickly.

"Of course you can. We're partners in this."

The flight from Fort Lauderdale to Charlotte was uneventful. Maggie fell asleep before they even reached ten thousand feet. When she awoke to the sound of the landing gear engaging, her head was on Mike's shoulder, and the noise from the plane engine had changed from a low hum to a higher-pitched grinding.

"Well, hello, sleepyhead," Mike said, stretching the arm that Maggie had been using as a pillow.

"So sorry," she said, "I guess I was tired. I normally can't sleep on a plane."

"No trouble today." Mike smiled.

"Did I snore?"

He smiled again. "Maybe a little."

The driver of the transfer van stood waiting at baggage with a sign that had *BS S&L* written boldly on a white piece of paper fastened on a clipboard.

"Not just *B-S* this time," Mike said, smiling at Maggie, who shook her head.

"There's a lot of B-S, if you ask me."

She looked at the faces around her. They were the same people that had started out on this journey, and the same member of their group who had not been with the group at the beginning of the trip was missing at the end. The faces might have been the same, but the group had changed in five days. The excitement that had been present the first day in anticipation of their adventure had been transformed into quiet contemplation and exhaustion. Everyone would go back to their regular routines on Monday morning…everyone except Mike and Maggie.

The driver dropped David and Kimberly at their cars in the bank parking lot. He loaded their bags into their vehicles then got back into the driver's seat. He looked in the rearview mirror at the three silent riders.

As soon as Mike's house was in view, Mike broke the silence.

"You two up to a visit with Aunt Millie today?"

"I think that might be a good idea," Joanie said without turning around.

Maggie remained silent but shrugged her shoulders.

At Mike's house the driver unloaded the bags. Joanie took hers directly to the trunk of her car and took off. "See you there," she called out as she spun out of the driveway.

Mike stood, watching her drive out of sight.

"What's that all about?" Maggie asked.

"I honestly don't know, but I wish we could have arrived together in a show of force."

"Do you think she's up to something?" Maggie asked, noticing the concern on Mike's face.

"She's always up to something." He pulled both his bag and Maggie's bag through the back door of his house and re-locked it. "I guess we better go now."

When they reached Aunt Millie's house, Mike's aunt was sitting on one of the rockers near the center of the long front porch. Joanie sat in the rocking chair next to her. Both had a glass of tea set on a small white wicker table. Two empty glasses and a half-full pitcher were waiting for them.

Aunt Millie smiled and waved as the two approached. "How was your trip?" She stood to hug Mike.

"I think you know how our trip went," Mike said, moving two of the rocking chairs to sit directly in front of her. She poured the tea into the empty glasses and handed one to Maggie and one to Mike. Joanie was gently rocking back and forth with one foot tucked under the other. Mike motioned Maggie to one chair. He took the other.

"Well?" he looked at his aunt and waited.

"You wouldn't understand, Michael. I am here alone every day bored to death. "

"Where did all the money come from?"

"It was all mine, but don't think I didn't consider 'borrowing' some from the crazy card ladies at the club."

"Why?" Joanie asked from her perch, as if she hadn't already filled her aunt in.

"They are always bragging about their children and grandchildren. They have everything, including plenty of money. I guarantee they wouldn't even notice the money was missing," she said.

"No, why did you set up such a scheme with your own money?" Mike asked.

"And how did you get John to go along with the plan?" Maggie asked.

"Everyone has secrets. You just need to know how to approach a man—or a woman, for that matter."

"Your aunt watches too much tv," Maggie said.

"Well, Ms. Maggie McFarlin," Aunt Millie said with a sly smile, "I know a lot more about you than you think."

Maggie sat back into the chair, hoping to escape any suspicion directed at her. "I have nothing to hide."

"Don't you?"

Maggie kept her composure, hoping that Aunt Maggie didn't know her secrets—how could she?

"Aunt Millie," Mike said. "This is about you, not about Maggie or me or even Joanie. It's about how on earth did you get an offshore account in the first place?"

"Darling, I've had that account for years."

"Who *are* you?" Joanie said, shaking her head.

"Why do you kids think old people are stupid? I have been on this earth a lot longer than you. I might have picked up a thing or two along the way. I figured you kids needed some adventure. Mike, what were you doing? Finding lost cats and spying on cheating husbands?"

"More cats than cheaters, unfortunately," Mike said.

"Seriously? Michael." Joanie gave her brother "the eye."

"I gave you a real case, and you solved it. No harm, no foul," Aunt Millie smiled, picking up the glass pitcher and pouring the remaining liquid into her glass. "More tea, anyone?"

"I could lose my job over this whole thing," Joanie said.

Millie tilted her head at Joanie. "Because I took out my own money?"

Joanie uncrossed her arms.

"Seriously, Joanie, look at your brother. I haven't seen him this happy in years."

"Oh, God, Auntie." Joanie shook her head.

"So, what happened to John?" Maggie asked.

"Aw, yes, John is fine. He is somewhere in St Lucia. I gave him a hundred thousand dollars, and he had some more stashed away; he is free from his ex-wife's clutches, and he's living in paradise. Now you want to talk about an evil ex-wife. He really had a doozy."

"The cruise line knows he survived," Mike says.

"Even better, since he is alive, the ex can't get the life insurance policy, win-win."

"But the—" Joanie started

"You are worrying too much," Aunt Millie interrupted her. "All the money in the bank here and all the money in the Cayman account will eventually be yours. Probably sooner than later. No one was hurt—so go ahead, admit it, this was fun."

She took a drink of her tea.

"I think you're a crazy old woman," Joanie said, "but I love you."

"Love you too," Aunt Millie said.

"Don't think we've finished this conversation, Aunt Millie, but I'm going to get Maggie back home. We'll talk later."

"All right, kids, see you later."

Aunt Millie stood and hugged Mike then winked at Maggie as they left.

*

"You're welcome to stay for a few days," Mike said to Maggie as they parked in his driveway.

"I think that would be a little awkward with your daughter, and honestly, I just need a hot bath and a bottle of wine."

"I understand."

Mike seemed a little disappointed, which surprised Maggie. She was sure his offer was made out of politeness rather than anything more emotional. He had made it clear that their relationship would remain a close friendship even after the kiss they shared. She had agreed deep down that there was no future between them except as friends.

They remained silent as Mike loaded Maggie's suitcase into the back of her SUV. Then they hugged goodbye.

"Stay safe on the road and call me before you head out, okay?" Mike had her by the shoulders.

"Absolutely," she said, smiling as she moved away from him. He held her door open as she buckled her seatbelt, and then he shut the door. With a small wave, she backed out of the driveway, leaving him standing there. She smiled weakly, wondering if she would ever see Mike Marker in person again.

*

Maggie woke up with a start, unfamiliar with her surroundings at first, but then remembering she was back at the Courtyard in Salisbury, North Carolina. Her phone was playing her default ringtone. She looked at the clock by the side of the bed: seven a.m. She looked at the phone again and saw it was one of her oldest friends, Katherine Frazier, from Bremerton, Washington. "Hey, what's up, Kat?"

"Maggie, it's Liza, she's in trouble."

"What do you mean she's in trouble?"

"Your sister killed her husband…Well, she didn't kill her husband. I mean, she said she didn't kill her husband, but she's in jail for killing her husband." Kat was rambling, and Maggie was shaking her head, trying to understand. She was still in a fog from her sleep.

"Kat, Kat…stop. Are you saying Trace is dead?"

"Yes, Trace is dead."

"And Liza is being accused of causing his death."

"Yes, and she needs you."

"Did she ask for me?" Maggie was confused. She was pretty sure she would never speak to her sister again.

"Of course she asked for you, that's why I'm calling."

"Okay, I'll be on a plane as soon as I can. Tell Liza I'm on my way."

Maggie stood paralyzed as she hung up the phone. Her sister was in jail…the same sister who had turned her back on Maggie ten years ago. That was all in the past, and now she needed Maggie's help.

Whether she liked it or not, Maggie knew she would finally have to face her past.

If you enjoyed this book please consider posting a review on Amazon. Even if its just a few sentences, it would be a huge help.

https://www.amazon.com/gp/product/B085X2Z5MT?notRe-directToSDP=1&ref_=dbs_mng_calw_0&storeType=ebooks#customerReviews

Authors Note

This is a work of fiction. Names, characters, businesses, places, events, locales, and incidents are either the products of the author's imagination or used in a fictitious manner. Any resemblance to actual persons, living or dead, or actual events is purely coincidental.

BOOKS BY THIS AUTHOR

Behind The Gates

A Maggie McFarlin Mystery-Book 1

Banyan Tree Country Club located in Boca Raton, Florida is an unlikely setting for a murder but when Marco Escobaris found dead, an arrow burried deep in his chest, Maggie McFarlin and her two lushy friends decide to investigate.

Even when Detective Mike Marker warns the women to stay out of the investigation, they continue their involvement exposing the motives of a colorful cast of suspects that lead the reader through several twists and turns along the way. It is a fast paced whodunnit. Can you guess who killed Marco Behind the Gates?